"What are you doing, Antonio?"

"Taking a chance that you are as unhappy with the just friends thing as I am," Antonio said, keeping his hand on her hip. He could feel Izzy's body heat and wanted to be closer. Wanted to lift the skirt on that flouncy dress of hers and slip his hand up underneath it.

"I am," she said, whispering the words so he had to strain to hear them. "I'm so torn right now. I can't stop thinking about you, Playboy. I can't figure out if being lovers would fix the problem."

"It can't hurt," he said.

"I hope you're right," she said, looking up into his eyes.

He was taking a risk. Hell, so was she. But he knew that denying himself Izzy wasn't helping his chances. He wasn't making rookie mistakes, but only because he had been lucky.

She distracted him, and he couldn't let her continue to do so...

Dear Reader,

I can't believe that this is the last book in the Space Cowboys series! It feels as if we were just getting started with Ace and Molly. This book is particularly close to my heart because Izzy Wolsten—female astronaut—gets to live out my dream of going into space.

When I was growing up we had these School Years books that included a spot for your yearly school photo, a chance for you write in who your friends were and which classes you liked best, and on the back of the page there were little check boxes separated into a column for boys and girls. In the boys section there were things like doctor, astronaut and firefighter, and on the girls section there was mom, teacher or secretary. The selection was limited for both genders but I always crossed off the word *boy* and wrote *girl* over it and checked *astronaut*. :)

Izzy and Antonio are both competing to be a part of the CRONUS mission, and more than that they want to be named to a crew that they know will be going to space. That first mission is very important to them because despite all of their training, not all astronauts make it into a final mission to space.

Thank you for reading this series and coming along with me on my own space odyssey.

Happy reading!

Katherine

Katherine Garbera

Beyond the Limits

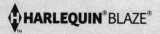
HARLEQUIN® BLAZE®

Recycling programs
for this product may
not exist in your area.

ISBN-13: 978-0-373-79968-8

Beyond the Limits

Copyright © 2017 by Katherine Garbera

Printed in U.S.A.

USA TODAY bestselling author **Katherine Garbera** is a two-time Maggie Award winner who has written more than seventy books. A Florida native who grew up to travel the globe, Katherine now makes her home in the Midlands of the UK with her husband, two children and a very spoiled miniature dachshund. Visit Katherine on the web at katherinegarbera.com, or catch up with her on Facebook and Twitter.

Books by Katherine Garbera

Harlequin Blaze

One More Kiss
Sizzle

Space Cowboys

No Limits
Pushing the Limits

Holiday Heat

In Too Close
Under the Mistletoe
After Midnight

Harlequin Desire

Baby Business

His Instant Heir
Bound by a Child
For Her Son's Sake

To get the inside scoop on Harlequin Blaze and its talented writers, visit Facebook.com/BlazeAuthors.

All backlist available in ebook format.

Visit the Author Profile page at Harlequin.com for more titles.

Nothing in life is possible without a really sturdy foundation, and I am so blessed to have been given that by my parents, so this one is for Charlotte and David Smith for always encouraging me to dream big and reach for the stars.

Acknowledgments

Special thanks to Dana Hopkins for guest editing the last two books in this series.

1

AT SIX FOOT ONE, Antonio "Playboy" Curzon immediately drew the eye. Isabelle Wolsten tried to look at him objectively. His muscles rippled and bulged with each upward motion of the weight bar he was bench-pressing, while a low, gravelly grunt captured way more than just her gaze. His short, spiky hair was drenched with sweat and stood up away from a perfectly formed scalp. He had a day's worth of stubble on his jaw and his dark brown eyes were intense as he continued his workout.

Aggravated with herself for even noticing, she pushed the button on the AlterG treadmill she was working out on to increase her bone density. She was one of eight women in the Cronus candidate class, and she was determined not lose her head over a pretty face.

But, damn, Playboy was more than a pretty face. He was a sexy, muscled, rock-hard body with a drawling Spanish accent. He was all the things her mother had warned her to watch out for and everything that her secret self wanted.

But could she really want him as much as she wanted to go to space?

Her snarky inner voice had been her guiding star all these years. Getting into NASA had been hard. At five foot two she was at the bottom end of the height requirement. She was wicked smart—no sense in denying it— and had been determined to make her mom's sacrifices count. Her mom had been sure that Izzy was meant for great things. She'd worked hard—an administrative assistant by day and an exotic dancer by night—and she'd saved every penny. Made sure they lived in the right neighborhoods and that Izzy went to the best schools. Her mom had endured all kinds of snide remarks so Izzy could be where she was today.

One of an elite class of sixteen who were in the final running to fill out the last three spots on the first long-term Cronus mission. She was proud of that. Really, she was. Which was why she wasn't going to let that hot body bench-pressing 250 pounds distract her.

It didn't matter that he smelled good. That his aftershave—probably something custom-made—had her thinking of long, sultry summer nights. She hit the off button before she lost her concentration and tripped over her own feet on the treadmill. She didn't look his way as she walked to the refrigerator that was packed with water and electrolyte-heavy beverages. Everything at the Mick Tanner Cronus Training Facility was to enhance an astronaut's ability to stay longer in space. They worked out for twice the amount of time the astronauts heading to the International Space Station did. They ate a diet that was rich in vitamins to enhance bone density, and they were monitored for the development of kidney stones.

Music was blaring through the speakers, some kind of death metal that their second-in-command, Thor, had put on to get the blood pumping. Izzy had just missed out on that position, but, despite that, she still wasn't a shoe-in for the first mission. Izzy finished her drink and moved over to the punching bags in the corner. She wrapped her hands and then put on the gloves, slowly finding her balance again. She wasn't going to let Antonio rattle her, even if he'd earned his moniker honestly. They'd been in the same candidate training class more than eight years ago. He'd been this born-with-a-silver-spoon guy who had too much charm and had bought his way in, while she'd gone to the academy on a merit scholarship and a recommendation from her senator.

She wasn't being fair—she knew that. He'd always been a hard worker, but he'd had an easier path and she resented it. He'd left NASA and gone into the private sector to join Space Now, a company owned by a billionaire who was innovating outside of NASA. She'd thought she'd seen the last of him.

Yeah, sometimes that chip on her shoulder showed itself a little more than she'd like. But she couldn't help it. She'd worked for everything she had. Rich guys like Playboy seemed to just waltz through life like it was nothing at all.

"Want me to hold the bag?"

That voice. He spoke English way better than she'd ever be able to master Spanish. And his accent—well, damned if it didn't undo all the resolve she'd just spent the last fifteen minutes shoring back up. She wasn't going to fall for him. She'd been strong when she'd gone through basic training. Ignored his flirting then, and she'd do it again now.

Except this time it was harder. She was more mature. Not as angry at the world as she'd once been, and Antonio…it seemed like experience had taught him a few things, too.

"Sure," she said.

She didn't say another word, instead picturing his strong jaw and dark brown eyes right in the center of the punching bag, and just went for it. Punched down the desire for him. Made herself believe there was nothing between them but sweat and—oh, hell, why did sweat smell so good on him?

This wasn't working. She dropped back and let her arms, which felt like noodles from the pummeling she'd just given the bag, drop to her sides. He watched her the way he always did.

The intensity in his stare made her feel that he could see past all her barriers. Past the workout clothes and the prickly exterior she used to keep everyone at arm's length.

"Why do you do that?" he asked.

"Do what?"

"Look at me like I'm your enemy," he said.

She shook her head, dropped her gaze and cursed herself inwardly. She turned away from him and used her teeth to loosen her boxing gloves. "Don't flatter yourself, Playboy, the only thing you see in my eyes when I look at you is a desire to make sure I stay one step ahead of you."

Yeah, right, and not a desire to see if his potent sexuality was the real deal or just another one of those things that looked better in the window. She walked over to the tablet mounted in the wall as she got first one and then the other glove off. Congratulating herself for leaving the encounter relatively unscathed, she entered her workout information, not paying attention to the fact that Antonio had followed her. He put his hand on the wall next to the tablet.

Even his forearm was too muscled and masculine. She doubted this man was going to have any problems with bone density. He was six feet one inch of Grade A prime male.

"It's not flattery, Bombshell. I know you keep watching me," he said. "Deny it all you want."

Isabelle Wolsten had haunted his dreams for more than eight years. Her icy gray eyes and platinum-blond hair just caught his attention. Wherever he was. But he hadn't set his sights on outer space just to be derailed by Izzy. She'd always been a distraction for him, probably because of the no-trespassing signs she kept firmly in place. So when she gave him her *not interested* glare, he'd respected it.

Their careers had taken them in different directions. She'd stayed within NASA and completed her training, and she'd been up to the ISS once. Antonio had taken a job with a private space firm, one that had allowed him to progress nicely and qualify for the Cronus missions. But he'd never been to space.

The Cronus missions and the later Mars missions would all be joint programs combining astronauts from NASA, international programs and privately-funded programs. Antonio suspected that the Cronus training facilities around the world would be as rigorous as this one, to ensure all of the astronauts were at the same high skill level.

He kept his body in top physical form at all times. He knew how demanding living in microgravity could be. Normally he had no problems keeping his eye on the end game, but Izzy… It was hard to think of her as Bombshell, which was her official call sign, or Ice Queen, which was what the men called her behind her back. He only thought of her as Izzy. The girl he'd first met when he'd arrived in Houston and been a little bit overwhelmed by everything. His English hadn't been as good back then, and the few conversational words she'd shared with him in Spanish those first weeks of basic training had been a balm.

It was only as they'd both continued to progress through the program and lust had reared its head that things had changed. He'd flirted and she'd diverted his attention. He'd dated other astronaut candidates and a few of the staff, and everyone had called him a playboy. He hadn't minded because the other guys said it with a kind of awe in their voices and the women… Well, it seemed to turn them on. But not Izzy.

She'd always kept her distance, which made him even more aware of her. She seemed not to notice him.

And though he was a grown man, a part of him wanted to do some crazy attention-grabbing stunt to make her react to him.

As much as he lifted weights to keep his body in top condition, he also did it because he knew she watched him. Ignoring her at twenty had been one thing, ignoring her now…well, he didn't want to do it anymore.

If everything went as planned, he would be spending most of his life outside of Earth's gravity. If she were interested, it would be counterproductive to ignore their sexual chemistry.

But she wasn't interested.

Still.

Even after eight years, she didn't want him. He knew he needed to let it go.

Which he totally would, if she didn't look at him sometimes with fire lurking just beneath the surface of those gray eyes of hers.

He turned away from her and walked back to the bench where he'd been working out. Better to concentrate on things he could control. Like the 250-pound weight bar and his reps.

He straddled the bench, refusing to look at the corner where he'd left Izzy, and leaned back. He closed his eyes as he took the smooth metal bar in his hands and inhaled before lifting it off the rack and over his head.

His muscles strained and he counted to ten in his mind before slowly lowering the bar to his chest. Again he did a ten count and lifted.

"I'm not denying anything, Antonio," she said. Her

nearness, her voice, startled him and the bar started to shift in his grip.

She straddled his chest and put her hands in the center of the bar, helping him to steady it.

"I didn't mean to distract you."

He groaned. She was high on his chest to help him with the bar and that meant that his gaze naturally went straight between her legs. Where the fabric of her workout shorts was pulled tight and he imagined he could smell her feminine sweetness.

He closed his eyes for a moment, lifted the bar and set it back in the rack. When he opened his eyes, Izzy had stepped over his body and stood next to the bench. Her shorts hugged the curves of her hips and the tops of her thighs. His fingers tingled—dammit, actually effing tingled—with the need to reach out and touch her. To put his hand on her thigh and draw her back toward him.

Closing his eyes had been a mistake. Instead of clearing his mind, he was assaulted with images of a topless Izzy on his lap on the bench.

He groaned.

"Did you hurt yourself?" she asked. She came closer. The scent of her flowery perfume and natural body musk was stronger now, and when he looked up at her he saw concern in those gray eyes.

Not ice.

"No. Not unless you count lust as a medical condition."

She bit her lower lip and took a step backward. For the first time it occurred to him that Izzy wasn't running because she didn't want him—maybe she wanted him too much.

"Do you?" he asked, swinging his legs toward her and sitting up on the bench. "Is that why you watch me?"

"Do I what?" she asked, putting her hands on her hips, which only served to draw his gaze to her breasts and her tiny waist. "Lust is for people who don't know what they want."

"Really?"

"Yes," she said. "I'm not denying there is a certain… attractive quality about you, Playboy, but I know how to control myself around pretty boys."

He stood up, taking the towel from where he'd draped it next to his bench, wiping his face and putting it around his neck. She watched him and didn't say anything else. He couldn't take his eyes from her mouth as he walked toward her. It was full and pert looking, with that little indentation in her top lip and the full lower lip. Her mouth looked lush. The kind of mouth he could spend a long time kissing.

"You keep saying *boy* but, in your eyes, Isabelle, I can tell that you see me as a man. One that you want," he said.

"Only someone without discipline would be governed by—"

He stepped closer and put his finger on her lip. That tingle was back, spreading from his fingertip throughout his entire body. Damn.

"I know you aren't going to say I have no discipline." She arched one eyebrow at him and nipped at the tip of his finger—which sent a sexual shock right to his groin—before stepping back.

"I didn't think it really had to be said. I mean, I've been trying to get a good workout in and you seem to be distracted."

Distracted?

The woman had no idea. All she had to do was walk into the same room as him.

He was about to rise to the bait when he saw the sparkle in her eye. She was teasing. Ah, that explained so much and at the same time made him want her all the more.

"I'm a team player. One of the philosophies of this training facility. You just went over to help me for your own good."

She shook her head. "Okay, if that's the way you want to play it."

"Are we playing?" he asked, but he knew they were. Maybe it was the fact that they were alone. Or even that they had been at the top of the class of candidates during the last training program. Everyone knew the two of them were going to be competing for the top spot. That one spot as payload specialist. Though there were two other spots, there was only room for one payload specialist which meant either Izzy or Antonio.

He took a step toward her and this time, instead of retreating, she closed the gap between them. Put her hand on his chest and held him there. "From the moment we met you've been flirting and acting like you were the bomb, and I let you because—"

"Because you knew I was, but you needed to focus on your training and on beating me," he said.

"Beating you? Playboy, I left you in the dust."

He leaned in closer, put his mouth next to her ear. "You only call me Playboy when I get too close to the truth."

She turned her head and he felt the minute exhalation of her breath across his cheek. She smelled like oranges and the first signs of spring, and this close, he saw her eyes were so much warmer than gray. They had blue and green flecks around the irises. Her lashes were thick and dark, and she had the tiniest mole under her left eye.

"What truth? That you're a man and I'm a woman?" she asked. "I thought you were smarter than that."

He laughed.

He couldn't help it. Every time he thought he had her figured out, she surprised him. He wasn't just drawn to her looks, which always made him catch his breath, but also her wit and her intelligence. She was the kind of person NASA wanted in command because she was the total package.

She made him want to be better. Not to best her but so he could stand shoulder to shoulder with her.

His laugh had surprised her and she turned her head back again so that their foreheads brushed and their noses were touching, and then her eyelids dropped to half-mast—and then he thought to hell with it.

What could one kiss hurt?

But as their lips brushed, that damned tingle moved through his body with all the precision and intensity of lightning on a dry field. He knew that he'd opened

Pandora's box. He pushed aside the warning bells and moved his mouth more completely over hers. Her fingers knotted in his shirt and tugged him closer, and then her lips parted under his. His tongue slid into her mouth, the taste of citrus so strong now.

Lightly he ran his fingers down the side of her neck and wrapped his hand around her shoulder, pulling her closer to him as she deepened the kiss, tilting her head, her grip on his shirt tightening. As if she'd never let go.

As if he'd never want her to let go, he thought. His mind screamed at him, *this is Izzy.*

Izzy.

Isabelle, who'd been one step ahead of him from the day they'd met. The truth dawned slowly as he realized that kissing her might be the biggest mistake he'd ever made. He'd thought not knowing how she tasted and felt in his arms was torture, but knowing and not being able to kiss her all the time was going to be even worse.

2

ANTONIO TASTED BETTER than chocolate cake on her birthday. He was forbidden and not good for her but, damn, he knew how to use his mouth. His body moved with the symmetry and precision of a well-oiled machine. She knew it had to be the result of all those hours he spent in the gym and on horseback.

He smelled…like a man. Not only of expensive cologne and whatever high-end retailers thought was masculine. Antonio was the real deal. He didn't hesitate when he kissed her, thrusting his tongue into her mouth and taking her completely. He gripped her butt, pulling her close, maneuvering his leg between hers until they were pressed together from the waist up. His chest moved against hers as he angled his head and pushed his hands into her hair. He held her head, positioning her for a kiss that left her completely under his spell.

She couldn't breathe or think. She saw stars as she closed her eyes and her hands went to his waist, clinging to his sides as he thrust his tongue into her mouth, mirroring the movement with his hips, rubbing his growing erection against her center and making her feel hotter than a rocket flying too close to the sun.

His lips were soft and supple as he moved them over hers. He took his time, seducing her, and she had to admit she liked it. Too often the guys she dated were aggressive, thinking they had to be because of her tough exterior. But not Antonio. He held her like he had all the time in the world.

She had to admit that scared her more than the fire burning through her body. Her breasts felt fuller and heavy, her skin sensitive even to her own clothes. She felt sensual, full of desire, and she couldn't help arching her back and feeling his hand on her backside as he tightened his fingers.

A meteor shower of sensation spread throughout her body and she tangled her tongue with his, sucking his tongue deeper into her mouth as she felt that need, that ache between her legs. She rubbed herself over him, but it wasn't enough. She wanted more.

She sucked harder on his tongue, trying to take control. Lifting her arms, she held his face, feeling his soft skin even as his stubble abraded her fingers. She rubbed her fingertips over it and then moved her hands slowly to his back, looping them around his neck.

Antonio kissed like he did everything else, with skill and accuracy, mastering her. And she was caught up in the maelstrom. Caught up in Antonio.

Suddenly she pulled back, breaking the kiss. This was the reason she'd stayed away from him. Not because of his reputation or the damage he could do to hers, but because of this. The overwhelming way he consumed her body and—if she wasn't very careful—her soul.

She tried to slip away but he held her with one hand at the small of her back and the other tangled in her hair. "I never figured you for someone who would back down."

His voice was sexy, his Spanish accent and the low husky timbre making her nipples harden and her center soften. She wanted him. Everything about Antonio was seductive, and now that she was in his arms, her willpower was gone.

But she had to own this. Couldn't let Antonio know how much power he had over her. She had to up the ante, press her advantage. Could she do it?

She had no choice because she knew if she walked away now, he'd always have beaten her. And that wasn't something she was willing to live with.

Maybe it only felt different with Antonio because he was tender yet dominant. There was no doubt that he was in complete control. And that was where her struggle lay.

She wanted to take control, but it felt good to just be in his arms, kissing him, not trying to prove she had the lady balls to own this moment. His hand trailed along the side of her neck, feathering his fingers against her until gooseflesh spread down her arm, making her nipples tighten even more.

"*Querida*, your kisses promise greater pleasure than I have ever known," he said, leaning in to whisper. She felt the brush of his lips against her neck, and then he moved his mouth lower, biting so gently that she barely felt the edge of his teeth against the point where her neck and collarbone met. It was erotic and made her want to rip off first her clothes and then his.

She buried her fingers in the thick richness of his hair and closed her eyes. She wouldn't deny herself this moment with Antonio. It had been risky of her to challenge him physically, and now it was clear she wasn't as immune to him as she'd thought.

ANTONIO NEVER LET himself lose control. His seductions were practiced and he always kept his cool. But not with Izzy. He shouldn't have been surprised by his reaction—from the first moment they'd met he hadn't been able to get her out of his mind.

But a gym—an open gym—wasn't the place he'd have chosen for their first encounter. He wanted time to explore every one of her curves and to learn the details of how soft her skin was. She rocked against him and he hardened even more. His gym shorts were starting to feel too tight and he knew that no matter what his rational mind wanted, if he didn't move soon, he was going to push her ridiculously short shorts down her long legs and find his way into her body.

He looked around the room and saw the door that led to the private workout room. It wasn't monitored and it would give them a modicum of privacy.

"Wrap your legs around me," he said, hardly recognizing the guttural sound of his own voice. He was further gone than he wanted to admit.

She did as he asked and he crossed the room in record time, holding her against him with one arm while he fumbled to open the door with the other. Once inside, he pressed her against the closing door.

Izzy looked up at him, and in her eyes he read a tangle of emotions. Sex was complicated. Even when he thought it wouldn't be, it was. It was hard to get naked with someone and then go back to business as usual.

Was this a mistake he shouldn't make?

"Antonio," she said.

A shiver of pure desire snaked down his spine and his balls tightened. She hardly ever called him by his given name and he'd never realized what a difference it would make. There had been a note of longing in the way she'd said it.

He couldn't think anymore. He had to act. He lowered his head once again and rubbed his lips over hers. They were soft and full, slightly swollen from their earlier kiss, and she parted them for him. Her tongue thrust into his mouth and tangled with his as she grasped his shoulders like she didn't want to let him go.

He certainly wouldn't let her go. This might come back to haunt him, but right now he had his arms full of the woman who'd inhabited his dreams for almost a decade.

He loved the way she felt in his arms, undulating against him as the kiss deepened. He felt the fullness of her breasts against his chest and fumbled for the hem of her T-shirt, pulling it up over her head and tossing it on the floor. He skimmed his gaze down her torso, taking in her narrow shoulders, defined arms and her black sports bra. He saw the small marks that sweat had left under her breasts as he traced the scooped neck that minimized her fullness.

She unwrapped her legs from his waist and slid down his body to stand in front of him. She pulled him away from the door and reached behind him to lock it.

The room had yoga mats stacked in one corner and a weight bench in another. He drew her across the room to the weight bench and sat down on it. He spanned her waist with his hands and lifted her onto his lap.

"I believe this is where I was," she said, straddling him.

"Seems almost right," he said. Her skin was a creamy white alabaster that contrasted with his darker, olive tone.

She sighed and he glanced up. Their eyes met and again he couldn't read what she was thinking.

He started to speak, but she put her finger over his mouth, hushing him. She tugged his shirt over his head and tossed it aside and then pulled off her sports bra. Her breasts fell free, bouncing against her chest, and he reached up to cup them as she shifted against him. She wrapped her arms around his shoulders as he leaned forward, burying his face between her breasts and using his hands to lift them toward his mouth. He tongued first one nipple and then the other as she scraped her nails down his back. She rocked against him.

The fabric of his boxer briefs and gym shorts was too confining. He needed to feel her pressed against him with no barrier, so he lifted his hips, reaching between their bodies to free himself.

He pulled the inner seam of her shorts and panties

away from her delicate flesh so he could reach up and caress her warmth.

He stroked along her most intimate flesh and then let the tip of one finger dip inside her. She arched her back and thrust her breasts toward his face. He suckled her nipple as he thrust one finger inside her before slowly drawing it back out again.

She rocked her hips against him again, reaching between their bodies to find his cock and stroke it. She held him, moving her hand up and down until he felt he could go crazy from the pleasure. He tore his mouth from her breast as he realized...

"Izzy," he said, kissing the valley between her breasts and running his hands up and down her back.

"Yes?"

"I don't have a condom. Are you on the pill?"

SHE COULD USE this as an excuse to stop, but she didn't want to. She was on the pill, and this thing with Antonio was overdue. She was going to enjoy a hot afternoon of sex and then put it in a box and never visit it again.

"Yes. Don't worry about it," she said. She knew they were both clean because they went through a barrage of tests almost daily. And right now the one thing that was on her mind was getting naked and getting back on his lap. His cock was so big and full and it had been far too long since she'd had sex.

He said something in Spanish, which she didn't understand, but she saw the gratitude on his face and nipped at his bottom lip. She stood up and shucked off her shorts and underwear.

She felt his fingers between her legs and looked down to see him parting her and stroking her. Her legs went weak and she reached for his shoulder to steady herself. He wrapped one arm around her waist and lifted her onto his lap.

His tip was at her entrance, and as she looked down into those large brown eyes, she wondered how she could ever have thought that he was off-limits.

He pushed her. He always had, and for once she didn't think that was a bad thing.

She shifted again and felt him stretching the entrance of her body. He replaced his tip with a finger, pushing inside of her, and she tightened herself around it. Stars burst behind her eyes. She hadn't felt this good in a long time.

She leaned forward, her arms on his shoulders as she found his mouth and thrust her tongue deep inside.

She felt him add a second finger, stretching her. Sensations pulsed through her. Izzy wanted to be detached, to focus on the physical sensations and not who was touching her. But she couldn't. This was Antonio making her feel she was going to shatter into a hundred pieces. Antonio who controlled her every move.

She moaned and felt her inner muscles start to clench around him, riding his fingers as an orgasm rolled through her.

She took her mouth from his and reached between them, drawing his hand away and positioning his cock where she needed him. She shifted her weight, felt his hands on her butt, clenching her cheeks as she slowly lowered herself onto him. When he was fully embedded inside her, he groaned and held her tightly to him.

He kissed her deeply as she started to ride him. His tongue plunged in and out of her mouth following the rhythm his body set. He urged her to go faster, driving them both higher and higher.

She wanted this to last but knew that it couldn't. They'd waited too long for this moment, and both of them were desperate. They needed each other so urgently.

His hold on her became fiercer as he moved underneath her, urging her to ride him harder and faster still, thrusting up inside of her with determination. She arched her back as she felt her climax building again, his mouth on the fullness of her breast, then latching on to her nipple and sucking her deep into his mouth.

Everything inside her clenched and stars danced behind her eyelids as the sensation spread throughout her body and a second orgasm rolled through her. She dug her nails into his shoulders as he continued to pound into her.

He threw his head back and groaned as she felt him empty himself inside her. She ran her hands up and down his back as he thrust into her a few more times, and then he slowed, wrapping his arms around her waist and resting his head on her shoulder.

She held him, too, her fingers toying with the hair at the nape of his neck and her heartbeat slowly settling down.

She hoped that this would be enough and she could go back to comfortably ignoring him. She wasn't ready to deal with Antonio and the consequences this might have on her emotions.

Of course this had been a mistake. It couldn't happen again, even though her body was still pulsing, still wanting him. She wanted to curl closer to him, so, instead, she pushed him away.

"Izzy, baby, that was something else. I guess this just proves that good things are worth the wait," he said. There was a softness in his tone that made her want to stay, to lower her guard, but she knew she couldn't.

It wasn't like they could date. The powers that be weren't going to put a newly dating couple in space for eighteen months.

"Maybe," she said. She didn't want to discuss this. She climbed off him and turned her back to him as she dressed, pulling on her panties and shorts and then trying to put on her sports bra. It got tangled as she drew it over her head and she felt his hands on her back, unrolling the fabric and slipping the bra into place.

"Thank you," she said, not looking at Antonio. She had scanned the room for her shirt before she noticed it in his hands.

He held it out to her. She took it without a word and put it on.

"So…"

"So," she said. "I don't know what to say."

"Me, either," he admitted. "I wasn't expecting this, but it's more than just an itch that I wanted to scratch… What about you?"

She held her breath. She could say it was curiosity that had led her to have sex with him, or she could be honest, the way he'd been, and admit that he had always fascinated her. Even when they'd first become friends and then rivals, there was something about this tall, dark Argentinian that made her pulse race.

An alarm sounded and the emergency lighting kicked on before she could answer. A shaft of fear and relief surged through her. She'd much rather face a real-life emergency than the emotions that Antonio brought out in her. She and Antonio both raced for the door.

3

ANTONIO WAS OUT the door right behind Izzy. The gym was empty, but when they entered the hallway they saw a lot of the candidates spilling from the different training rooms. Everyone looked dazed. A smoky haze in the hallway made him worry about fire. The alarm was loud, and there was the sound of something crashing in the distance.

"Someone needs to take the lead," Izzy said. "And then we need to sweep the rooms to make sure everyone is out."

"I'll take care of this group," Antonio said. "You have more medical training than I do—why don't you go see if anyone is injured."

"Sounds good," Izzy said.

"Listen up, everyone," Antonio said. "We are going to stay together and leave the building. Bombshell is going to sweep the rooms to make sure everyone is out."

"Is she nuts? We should all just get out of here," one

of the candidates from the NASA team said. Antonio wasn't sure his name.

"There are only—" he broke off as he scanned the faces "—eight of us here. We know there are twenty-four candidates who could be in this building at any time."

"I'll help Bombshell," Velocity said. He was one of the senior astronauts in the program and Antonio had a lot of respect for him.

"Sounds good. Be safe."

Antonio looked at Izzy's heart-shaped face for just a moment too long. He wanted to grab her and take her out of the facility, but she was well trained and would be fine. She gave him a nod before heading into the room closest to them. She was doing her job; it was time for him to do his.

"Let's go. Follow me," Antonio said in a loud voice to command their attention. "Everyone move out."

He led the way down the corridor, keeping the group moving. He wished he could help Izzy check the rooms, but his focus had to be on getting the candidates to safety first.

"Cover your noses and mouths," he said, pulling his own shirt up to do so. The smoke was thicker as they proceeded down the hall. The scent was odd, more chemical than woody.

He tucked that fact away in the back of his mind to analyze later. One of the candidates from Space Now made a sort of panicked moaning sound and started to run. Antonio stopped the man with a hand on his arm.

He had to think for a minute to remember the candidate's name.

Peter Jensen. He was from the UK and had trained with their space program before joining Space Now two years ago.

"Jensen, stay centered. This is nothing to worry about. We are going to get out of here," Antonio said.

"I know… I know, man, but fire… It's one thing I have nightmares about. I'm not sure I can—"

"You can. We're all right here with you. And if we do this calmly and sensibly we can all get out of here together. There's no reason to panic. I won't leave you," Antonio said.

Jensen nodded, causing the shirt he had tied around his face to slip. Antonio stopped walking and gestured for the rest of the group to keep moving as he retied the shirt on the kid's head. "Let's go."

Everyone had stopped around the corner, and Antonio made his way to the front of the group to find debris that had fallen from the ceiling blocking their path. Three of their group were already working to shift it, and he and Jensen joined them. Antonio had a lot of training in working with people in emergency situations at home on the ranch in his native Argentina. And he knew from experience that giving people a task made them feel more in control of the situation.

So he gave a task to everyone who had hung back, getting the team to shift the pile of rubble and debris until they could all safely move through the hallway. Once again he found himself at the front of the pack, and as they neared the exit, he noticed that the smoke was getting thicker.

"Everyone down on the floor. We need to crawl," he said.

Everyone reacted quickly, following Antonio's lead. The smoke was thinner on the floor and he moved with as much speed as he dared, constantly monitoring the team by looking back over his shoulder and keeping a close eye on the floor ahead of them for new dangers.

They reached the exit and he touched the door with the back of his hand to see if it was hot.

It wasn't.

He slowly lifted himself into a standing position and opened the door. Fresh air rushed in as the smoke billowed out, and Antonio motioned for the candidates to leave the building. He stood by the door, counting to make sure the six people he'd had with him at the beginning of the journey were all here.

Though Antonio had expected to see emergency vehicles, there were none, just the open Texas landscape under the early-evening sky. He scanned the area again and noticed Jessie Odell, the survival instructor, standing to one side with Ace, the commander, and Thor, Ace's lieutenant for the mission.

He had a feeling this was a test and could only hope that he'd done enough to pass. Getting on the first Cronus mission was his goal. But he realized he was also worried about Izzy. He knew she could hold her own but if this were a test, who knew what might be waiting for her in the facility.

IZZY HAD TRAINED with Velosi, aka Velocity, for the last six months at this facility. They'd both been close to winning the second-in-command position that had ultimately gone to Thor. A part of her was glad for the screaming alarms and smoke filling the hallway, because it was much easier to deal with an emergency than to worry about the aftermath of making love with Antonio.

His call sign was Playboy.

That should have been enough for her to have stayed away. Sleeping with him might jeopardize her chances of making the Cronus mission, but that didn't stop her from remembering the way he'd felt inside of her with a delighted shiver.

"Want to split up?" Velosi asked. "You take the left and I'll take the right."

Focus, girl. This was what she was good at. She'd come so close the last time.

"Yes. Call out when you enter and leave a room," she said. "Velocity in. Velocity out. Room clear. Does that work for you?"

"Sounds good, Bombshell. Let's do this. I don't think my wife will be too happy if I end up getting hurt while I'm training in Texas."

Nor did she want to be injured and out of the game before they were even named for a mission. "I agree. We need to be quick and get moving."

There were three rooms on either side of the hallway that led to the back of the gym. The smoke was getting a little bit thicker and Izzy took off her shirt and tied it over the bottom half of her face. She carefully touched the door to check for heat before she reached for the handle. Only after she was sure it was cool did she call out that she was entering the room, turn the handle and go in. She scanned the room first, just as she'd been taught in her first emergency training class and then walked the perimeter, confirming it was empty.

She exited and called out, then waited for Velosi. He rejoined her soon after, and they confirmed their rooms were clear. They cleared the other two rooms before returning to the gym and starting toward the exit.

They worked efficiently. The third room she entered was different. As soon as she stepped inside she saw the smoke was thick in one corner. She dropped to her hands and knees and slowly worked her way around the perimeter, finding someone slumped near the back.

She rolled the person over; surprised to find it was Molly—Ace McCoy's fiancée and one of the people who liaised between the ranch and the training facility. The facility had been built on the Bar T ranch in the town of Cole's Hill, Texas a little over forty-five minutes from Houston. Out here they had the space to do the training. She leaned over Molly to see if she was breathing and felt a reassuring exhalation. She ran her hands along Molly's sides to make sure that there were no injuries or protruding bones.

Nothing broken, but she was unconscious.

She heard Velosi calling that he was clear.

"Woman down in here," she yelled. "Lots of smoke, so you'll have to crawl."

She shook Molly's shoulder, but she only made a moaning sound and didn't wake up. There were first-aid kits in all of the rooms, and as soon as Velosi announced that he was in the room she instructed him to bring the kit.

She continued to try to rouse Molly, relaying the other woman's condition to Velosi as soon as he reached her. She used the flashlight on her phone and found the smelling salts in the first-aid kit.

When she waved them under Molly's nose, the other woman jerked upright. "What's going on?"

Thank God. She had been scared for her friend. "You were unconscious. We don't know if it was due to the smoke or something else. Do you think you can walk?" Izzy asked her.

Velosi had checked the room for anyone else. "Were you alone in here?"

"Yes. Just finishing up my paperwork. I should be able to walk," Molly said.

"Good. Until we are out of this room you should crawl," Izzy told her.

"Follow Bombshell," Velosi said. "I'll be behind you."

Together they inched through the room and into the hallway. Izzy handed a bottle of distilled water from the first-aid kit to Molly while Velosi scouted up the hallway.

"There is a pile of debris that has been shifted and two more rooms. I don't like the idea of either of us being left alone in the building. Molly, are you okay to move slowly with us as we clear the last two rooms?"

"Yes. I'll be fine," Molly said.

They walked past the debris, and then Izzy waited

with Molly while Velosi checked out the room on the right and then he waited with Molly while she checked the right. The rooms were both clear and as they got closer to the door, they felt fresh air. Izzy guessed that Antonio had already gotten the rest of the candidates out.

She shouldn't have been surprised so many of them were in the building on a Sunday evening. Even though some of the candidates would be enjoying time off in the neighboring town of Cole's Hill, Izzy wasn't the only workaholic in the group.

Izzy put her arm around Molly's waist and Velosi flanked them as they stepped outside. She had expected to see an emergency team waiting but they were greeted only by the candidates and facility staff.

As soon as Ace saw Molly he ran over to put his arms around her. "What the hell were you doing in there?"

"Catching up on paperwork," she said.

Realization flared in Izzy, and so did her anger. "Good thing your people are so well trained," Izzy remarked. "Otherwise this *training exercise* could have ended in unforeseen tragedy."

ACE AND DR. TOMLIN took Molly to the side to examine her. The smoke had affected her, and some of the other candidates, too. Thor called for all of them to meet in an hour for a post mortem in the common room in Bunkhouse 1, which was where Antonio's rooms were located.

The candidates dispersed, but Izzy headed toward Thor with Velocity behind her. It didn't take a genius to figure out that the alarm was a test. Antonio noticed Jessie Odell making notes and he followed behind the other two to confront Thor.

"This is our day off," Izzy said. "I don't mind tests— I think they keep us all sharp—but on our day off? That's not right."

"Normally I'd agree," Thor said as Antonio joined the threesome. "But Cronus isn't like other missions. There are so many variables to be considered. Emergencies in a long-term mission might happen on your downtime."

Izzy put her hands on her hips and shook her head. "I get what you're saying, but that means that we can never let our guard down. That we are all effectively training 24/7."

"That's a big ask, Thor," Velocity said.

"I don't agree," Antonio added. "Some of the candidates are fresh recruits who have never been on a mission before. This test shook some of them and it's better to find out on the ground if someone can't cut it."

Izzy gave Antonio a hard stare over her shoulder. He had forgotten how fierce she could be when she was challenged.

"That's exactly why we are running these tests. You three are more experienced, but there are some candidates here who, frankly, are a gamble. We don't know yet what they are made of. They all passed rigorous qualifying tests, but stuff happens. Things go wrong. We need to know how each person will react. You three showed your mettle today," Thor said. "Now go and clean up and meet the team in the main area of Bunkhouse 1 at 1600 hours."

Thor walked away from the group and they all turned to head to the bunkhouses together. Velosi was in Bunkhouse 3, a new addition to the facility now that there were more candidates coming in. Velosi and Izzy had been on the Bar T Ranch for over six months. He'd volunteered to switch to the new bunkhouse in order to mentor a few of the newer mechanical-engineering candidates.

Antonio wanted to touch her and make sure she was okay. Pull her away from the others and hold her for a few moments. The emergency hadn't given them a chance to regroup after they'd made love.

"Izzy—"

"Don't. I am not ready to talk about anything," she said. "Except, why didn't you have my back when we were talking to Thor?"

What had happened between them had been hotter and more rare than a comet snaking past Earth, and she wanted to discuss a difference of opinion? Fine. He could do that.

"One of the guys in my group freaked a bit as we were leaving. It made me realize how inexperienced some of these candidates are. We were lucky to have our training before coming to this program," Antonio said. "Which is exactly what I said to Thor."

"Sorry. Finding Molly like that put me on edge. She was slumped over on the floor. That was so scary," Izzy said. She stopped walking and turned to face him, her gray eyes full of conflicting emotions. He reached for her, but she shook her head.

"No. We can't do the personal thing. We had sex. That's it," she said. "We've seen how intense it is here, and I'm pretty sure they aren't going to be too happy if we start something."

"That's it? Don't I get a say in this?" he asked.

"Sure," she said. "But I don't think you want to risk your chances of going on this mission. You know there are no guarantees for who will be chosen. And no matter how incredible we are together, we've both worked our entire lives to be on a mission like this."

She was stubborn, but he'd already known that. And she made a good point. The hot sex they'd shared had served to whet his appetite for her, but maybe it had cooled hers for him. Maybe that one time was all she needed.

It didn't seem possible that she could feel nothing for him when he wanted her so much. "I think Ace was freaked, too," Antonio said at last, following her change of subject. Retreat wasn't really his style, but if she needed time to process things he'd give it to her. He put his doubts aside. One time wasn't going to be enough... for either of them. And work was easier to discuss.

"He was," Izzy admitted. "She's not a candidate and doesn't have the training we do. I'm glad we got to her when we did."

"I agree," Antonio said. "I think it proves Thor's point that you can never be prepared for anything. They planned this drill but didn't know she'd get caught in the middle of it."

"Probably. It's just that we follow so many procedures and regulations with the program," she said. "We're in the same bunkhouse, right?"

"Yes."

She gave him a sideways look. "Why haven't I seen you in the common room?"

"That answer is complicated," Antonio said.

4

A SECRET.

She wasn't sure she wanted to know any more of Antonio's secrets. She already knew the way his body felt pressed next to hers and the sound he made when he came inside her. The way the scent of his aftershave mingled with sweat on his body and how easily he rattled her self-control.

The smart thing to do would be to walk away. But she was still on edge. Finding Molly had rattled her. The risks associated with space missions had always been high, though sometimes Izzy felt that modern innovation had made spaceflight safer.

But the explosion of the test rocket a few months ago had reminded her that those risks hadn't lessened. The stakes were high, so maybe, just for the moment, she could do something fun with Antonio.

Still, she wasn't sure if what he was offering was fun.

She had her guard up now. She had thought that it would be like blowing off steam, but it had been more—

just like everything with Antonio was. Which was why she found herself back in front of the bunkhouse after showering and changing into jeans and a T-shirt.

"What's this secret?" she asked as he walked over to join her.

He'd changed, too, and looked like the cowboy he was. He had on a pair of faded denim jeans that clung to his thighs and rode low on his hips. His boots were worn but good quality and he had on a button-down ranch shirt. He held a straw cowboy hat loosely in one hand and a bandanna was tied around his neck.

"Come with me and find out," he invited. He held his hand out to her and led her not toward the bunkhouses but away from the Mick Tanner facility and onto the path that led to the Bar T.

"Why are we going toward the ranch?"

"So I can show you why I haven't been hanging out in the common room," he said.

"And it's on the ranch?"

"Yes, ma'am," he said.

She smiled to herself. He sounded like the ranch hands on the Bar T. They all had good Southern manners, and it was sort of amusing to hear Antonio talking like them in his Spanish accent.

"I think I'm seeing the vaquero side of you," she said.

He gave her a half grin over his shoulder. "You might be. As much as I always wanted to be in the space program, there is also a part of me that loves the land and ranching. So when I have some downtime I've been working with the hands."

She was a step behind him and couldn't help noticing the way his jeans hugged his butt. She caught herself and blushed. "So what's the secret?" she asked.

He led her to the barn and down the aisle that was bordered with stalls on each side. He stopped in front of a stall that was labeled Arabella.

"Is this your horse?"

"Yes. I had her brought up here from my family's estancia," he said. "My brothers like to tease me about her name, but I picked it for a very specific reason. Can you guess?"

She walked into the stall with Antonio as he started running a brush over the sides of his horse. She was beautiful—even Izzy could see that and she wasn't really familiar with horses. Arabella. She ran the name through her mind, trying to come up with a connection that made sense. Then she remembered the two spiders that were part of early NASA experiments, spinning webs while weightless in space during the Skylab project in 1973. Anita…and Arabella.

"Skylab '73," she said.

"Very good," he said with a wink.

"So this is your secret?" she asked. "I think some of the other candidates that have ranching backgrounds have brought their horses."

"They have," Antonio said, putting the brush down as he walked around behind the horse to a pile of blankets in the corner. "This is my secret."

She came closer and noticed a small dog nestled in the blankets. The dog bounded to her feet as Antonio came closer, dancing around his legs as he bent to pet her.

"Who is this?"

"Carly. Near as I can tell she's a mix of dachshund and corgi. She just showed up during one of my morning rides and followed me back here. I'm waiting to hear back from Jeb about her staying on the ranch—do you know the foreman?—so I've been letting her bunk in with Arabella. But I have the feeling she was a house dog and not a ranch dog. She pretty much stays in the stall."

"So you are going for morning rides and you have a secret dog named Carly. Why did you pick that?" she asked. She wanted to keep Antonio at arm's length and this certainly wasn't helping. But realizing there was so much more to Playboy than she'd expected also helped distract her from her thoughts about the risks of spaceflight.

"It's short for Carletta, which means *manly*. I figured with such a silly little dog I needed something strong," Antonio said.

But the dog wasn't silly, Izzy thought as she watched Antonio stroke her. She'd only ever seen him as the competition or as someone to be avoided. But now she had a glimpse into the man…the man she'd made love with, and she realized that this might be more dangerous than fighting a fire.

ANTONIO HAD PLACED a quick call to his boss at Space Now while he'd been getting cleaned up. Unlike Izzy, he'd never been up on a mission, despite the fact that he'd been assigned to two and had been training for the better part of ten years. In the US only forty-eight astronauts had gone on long-term missions, and working within NASA, Antonio had quickly realized his chances of making it to space were minimal.

He'd used his family connections to the tech billionaire Malcolm Pennington to get himself a role as a senior astronaut with Space Now. He had the same training and skills as many of the NASA candidates; the field was simply smaller at Space Now.

Mal had been informed of the smoke test from Antonio and was en route to Texas to oversee this last phase of training and selection. He wanted to make sure as many of the Space Now candidates as possible were named to the Cronus missions.

Antonio was very aware of the fact that he and Izzy were going for the same role on the mission. And he thought that his employment with Space Now gave him an edge. After all, NASA had placed two of their candidates already on the team with Ace and Thor. The agencies outside of NASA who were equal partners in the financing and development of the mission wanted to have the same number of astronauts on the missions.

He glanced at his watch and realized they had twenty minutes before they were due back at the training facility for the debriefing.

"Want to help me groom Arabella?" he asked.

"I have been avoiding as much of the ranch chores as possible," Izzy admitted, pushing a strand of her platinum-blond hair behind her ear. "But grooming the horses is one that I don't mind."

He handed her one of the grooming brushes and went to fetch a second one for himself. She worked on one side, he on the other.

"Why is that?" Antonio asked after a few minutes had passed. He loved the sounds of the barn. As a child he'd spent many hours grooming his horse, thinking of the future and dreaming of being in space.

"I could name the physical benefits of working out with one arm, but that's not why I do it. There is something so soothing about standing here and looking after horses. I like the smell of the barn, all leather and hay—"

"And other scents," Antonio reminded her. But he liked it, as well. As soon as he stepped into the barn, his other worries left. He was grounded here as much as he was when he got into the simulator at Space Now.

"Sometimes," she admitted. "But most of the time it's so solitary. Just me and the horse and the sound of the brush as I move it over her coat. And it gives me time to think and analyze whatever problems we've been dealing with at the facility. Working this way helps to soothe me."

"Me, too," he admitted. "Sometimes I think you and I have a lot in common."

She looked over at him with those wide gray eyes of hers. "Some things. But when the trainees for the NASA program swelled in number, you were able to leave to go to a smaller private company…"

"Are you jealous?"

"Sure. Who wouldn't be? I want to log as many hours in space as I can," she said.

"You don't think you're a shoo-in?" he asked. Honestly, he did feel at a disadvantage that he was just joining the Cronus training program here in Texas. He was pretty sure that many of the other new candidates felt the same way.

"No one is. I think today just proved how high the bar is being set. What if that alarm had gone off ten minutes sooner?" she asked. "We both would have been…"

"In a very delicate position," he said. He didn't regret his intimate time with Izzy—how could he? He'd spent years dreaming of having her in his arms. And if today had proved anything, it was that the bond between them was a strong one. At least physically.

"Exactly. I don't want to take a chance on screwing up. Even though I do feel like you took the easier path—" she held up her hand to stop him from responding "—we both have worked too hard to jeopardize our shot at getting on this mission."

"I agree. We have worked hard. What are you trying to say?" he asked.

"That we keep our distance. Work together as we have to in the training sessions, but no more—" She gestured to the two of them, her hand going back and forth.

"I don't know what that means," he said, curious that a woman who was truly one of the boldest, bravest people he knew was trying to avoiding saying anything intimate.

"It means no more hooking up," she said.

He bit the inside of his cheek to keep from smiling. "Fair enough. You know, you came on to me."

She put her hands on her hips and gave him a hard glare, and then she threw back her head and laughed.

"I did, didn't I? I thought that if we cleared the air we'd be able to work better together. I never expected it to go so far."

"I did," he admitted. From the moment he'd seen her, she'd been a fire in his blood, and nothing had changed that. "But from now on, we can keep our distance."

"Yes," she said. "I think I'm done grooming this horse."

"Vaquero, you in here?"

"*Sí*, I'm back here," Antonio answered.

Jeb, the ranch foreman, poked his head around the stall and leaned in. "Ma'am. Antonio, I could use a hand with some fence repair if you have the time. And I talked to Ace—you can keep Carly in your room at the bunkhouse for now. We are looking around in town to find her owners."

"I have a meeting at 1900, but I think I could help out for a little while," Antonio said.

He glanced over at Izzy, who was simply watching him and Jeb. "Wanna help?"

"No" WOULD HAVE been a perfectly acceptable answer, Izzy reminded herself as she held a length of fencing in place as Antonio hammered a nail to fix it. The setting sun shone brightly and it felt good doing something instead of being back in her room remembering that scary moment when she'd found Molly.

She kept getting flashes in her mind of finding her friend's slumped body in the corner of the room. And the acrid smoke that she'd breathed in seemed to burn the inside of her nostrils every once in a while.

"Izzy?"

"Yes?" she asked, glancing toward Antonio. His hands were on his hips and he was watching her. He looked good dressed as a cowboy. Some of the other candidates looked like they were playing dress-up, but he wore the clothes with a natural air that made him seem a part of this landscape.

"I said that's it. Are you ready to head back?" he asked.

She nodded and turned toward her horse but stopped. "I keep thinking about Molly. What if something like that had happened in space?"

She didn't hear Antonio move and jumped when he put his hand on her shoulder. "We'd cope with it, same as we did today. But it is scary. We have to be able to rely on the team completely."

"Exactly. I mean I know Velocity really well, so I'm happy to have him at my back, but some of these people…how are they going to make us into a team?"

"With a lot of hard work," Antonio said.

"Do you know the people from Space Now well?" she asked. She'd worked with everyone who had come through NASA, or else she knew them by their reputations. She'd read the dossiers on all of the new candidates, as she assumed they'd done with her, but she'd worked with very few of them and hadn't even heard of some of them.

Antonio echoed her thoughts. "Some of the Space Now candidates are new, people I haven't worked with, but most of them I know. They were rigorously vetted before being sent here."

She put her hand up. "I wasn't judging them. I was thinking more from my own perspective. It's hard to build trust. I imagine that's what Thor and Ace are going to be trying to get us to do while we learn how to use the equipment that we will need to build the way station."

"It will work out," he said.

She turned to face him, caught between him and her horse. She looked up at his tanned face, hidden from the sun under the brim of his straw cowboy hat. He had deep laugh lines around his eyes, and his eyelashes were thick. His eyes as he watched her seemed cautious. But then, maybe she was projecting that onto him since she wanted to be watchful around him. Careful not to let him slip past her guard again.

What if it doesn't work? But she didn't ask him. Instead, she just closed her eyes, which was a mistake. The sun disappeared and she flashed to the hallway filling with smoke, hearing echoes of the alarm. Her eyes popped open and she saw that Antonio was studying her.

He put his hand under her chin and looked down at her with an expression she'd never seen on his face before. It was tender and almost sweet, and it made her realize that she'd made more than a basic mistake in letting him in. She'd made a critical error. The kind that could cost lives in space and, if she wasn't very careful, possibly her place on the Cronus mission.

She pulled back, turning away from him and trying to mount up. She got her foot in the stirrup, and the ranch-trained horse stood still as she tried to use her arms and a hop to get up in the saddle.

He cursed under his breath in Spanish, which somehow sounded more elegant than it did in English. He put his hand on her butt and gave her a boost up into the saddle. She swung her leg over and seated herself before turning to thank him. He'd already sauntered over to his horse.

Arabella.

The horse named after one of the spiders NASA had sent into space. She realized the stakes were high for Antonio, as well. She had to remember that. Sleeping with him hadn't just affected her. Antonio was going to have to deal with the fallout, too, and if the way he clicked his heels and started galloping across the open field was any indication, he was as frustrated as she was with the attraction that was still there between them.

5

"THANK YOU ALL for meeting back here. Ace is with Molly, who will be fine, but he didn't want to leave her alone. She suffered some low-level smoke inhalation," Thor said as he addressed all of the candidates.

Izzy stood in the back next to Velosi and some of the others who'd been here since the beginning. She and Velosi had been at the Mick Tanner Training Facility since day one and they were familiar with the program. But today the stakes had been raised. Sundays were downtime. Everyone knew that.

Not anymore.

The smoke hadn't been an accident. It had been a test. And while Izzy had no problem participating in tests and honing skills, she did think it was a little sneaky of Thor, Ace and program director Dennis Locke to have implemented this one the way they had.

Dennis stepped up next to Thor. Dennis was in his fifties but was fit and looked younger. His hair was graying at the temples but his gaze was still as sharp as his early mission photos when he'd been in his twenties. Izzy respected him and felt fortunate to be included in a program that he was heading up.

"I know that some of you have raised concerns about the test happening on your day off, and I've addressed most of you privately. But I do want to say publicly that from this point forward every day—even your down ones—will be some sort of training," Dennis said.

"They could have mentioned that earlier," Velosi said under his breath. "But let's face it, we know you don't get a day off in space."

"So true," Izzy said.

"Many of you have met the candidates who have joined us from the international and privately funded space programs like Space Now, but until today you didn't have the chance to see each other in action. While the emergency situations occurred at the three locations where we had staff—the training facility, bunkhouses and the ranch pasture—you all were challenged in different ways."

Thor stepped forward. "We felt it was necessary to see if you all could function as a team without us making you into a team first. These exercises were very successful and we have identified the candidates who have already made a strong impression."

Dennis spoke again. "As you know, you are all qualified and have unique skills, but the first mission will be the one where we anticipate the most unforeseen problems, and that is why we have been training, testing and slowly building that first crew. The subsequent missions will be built on new knowledge."

"We are going to divide you into two teams of twelve and each of you will be challenging yourselves within the group and against the other team," Thor continued. "You will select a leader for yourselves and you will start to work completely with that team. You will eat together, do the ranch chores together, train together... In effect, you will be a unit."

"Dr. Tomlin has a bowl with twelve red and twelve blue markers. Please come forward and select one to determine your team," Dennis said. "Blue team, you will be rotating to the ranch for two weeks for intense team building, muscle building and general skills. Red team, you will be in the facility for two weeks in the new rocket simulator that has just been installed."

Izzy felt a tingling in her stomach. The mission was becoming more real. From the moment she'd arrived in Cole's Hill, she knew that the end goal was the way station in orbit halfway between Earth and Mars, but it had seemed so far away. Now that they had the rocket simulator that would mirror the actual vessel that would take them to the location where they would assemble the way station...she was getting excited.

She looked around for Antonio and noticed he stood with a group of astronauts from the EU. He caught her gaze and winked at her. She just shook her head. She was glad that she'd had her little lapse in control where he was concerned before this announcement. She hadn't had time to change when they'd come back from their ride, but she was determined to keep her distance from him.

She was happily going to tuck Antonio back into the box marked off-limits and focus on the Cronus missions. Not that she hadn't been before, but now that the missions were getting closer, she knew there was no room for error. And sleeping with Playboy had definitely been an error.

But it was in the past. Maybe they'd be on different teams and they'd hardly see each other.

Please let us be on different teams, Izzy thought as she walked up to the bowl behind Velosi and drew out her marker. It was blue. Velocity's was red. He shrugged and walked over to the red group. Izzy did the same, joining the other blues.

She chatted with the candidates on her team, trying to appear as if she wasn't paying attention as Antonio moved closer and closer to the bowl to make his selection. She looked deliberately away from the selection line and yet couldn't help glancing back as his big hand reached into the bowl and pulled out the blue marker.

Damn.

No, not damn. She could handle this. It was better to have him in close working conditions so she could prove to them both he wasn't going to distract her. She could handle anything NASA, the Cronus team and life threw at her.

Even a six-foot-one, sexier-than-hell astronaut.

"Looks like fate wants us together," Antonio said as he took a spot next to her.

She wanted to say something to put him in his place, to challenge him and shut him down all at once. But words escaped her and she could only nod. "I think that we are going to be working really hard, and neither one of us wants to let this moment pass us by," she said pointedly.

ANTONIO HAD HOPED to be on the same team with Izzy because he knew he'd perform better with her so close. She challenged him, and earlier when they'd both been working to get all of the candidates out of the facility, he'd realized how much he trusted her. That was very important.

He had the feeling she was going to keep him out of her bed, but he wanted to convince her otherwise. He wasn't done exploring the sensuality that had always been between the two of them. Now that he'd held her in his arms, he wasn't ready to let go.

Thor and Dennis stepped forward. Dennis said, "Ace will be the point person for the red team, but for this afternoon I will be filling in. Thor is the contact for the blue team. We will start the new team rotations in the morning. Tonight there is a barbecue at the lake and I give you all my word that there will be no more tests today. Let's take fifteen minutes to meet with your teams."

Dennis stepped to one side, leading the red group out of the common area and over to Bunkhouse 2. Thor waited until he was gone and then gestured for everyone to sit down.

"All right, team, this is how it's going to work. There will be more of these pop-up experiences over the course of the next eight weeks. We will be rotating back and forth between the facility and the ranch. The main idea for this is to expose you to physical labor that tests different muscle groups and to see how you work outside of the rocket together. Eventually the way station will house several hundred staff, and we will need skills that go beyond your ability to operate at your station."

"If we are on the ranch first does that mean we won't be working on the simulator?" Antonio asked.

"You will have an opportunity to tour the simulator tomorrow between the ranch duties. You will be eating together as a team and continuing your lessons at the facility, and I have a revised schedule here. For the first few days you will be observed and then we will pick a handful of you to be leaders. The teams will need to have commanders rotating on and off duty and it's important for you to remember that no matter what role you are chosen for, it's how well you perform that counts in the end."

Of course it was. Antonio's bosses at Space Now were concerned that NASA might try to stack the deck in their favor. To choose their trained candidates over the other ones. It was paramount that he use all of his abilities to ensure he was at the top of this group.

Which was exactly what he would do. Keeping his personal and professional life separate was a specialty, but no doubt Izzy was too much of a distraction. At first he'd thought the challenge of having Izzy on his team would spur him on but now he was having second thoughts. What if she distracted him? Should he ask to be moved to the other team?

Or would that be perceived as a weakness?

For as long as he could remember he'd wanted to get away from his family's ranch in Argentina. He didn't like to dwell on the incident that had caused him to leave his family and the land they loved so much, and he didn't let his mind go there now. As much as his father and brothers had loved the land, Antonio had loved the stars. He'd spent all of his time reading books about planets and cosmology, dreaming of a time when he'd be up in the stars and far away from cattle and horses.

The irony of this facility setup wasn't lost on him. Of course he had to make peace with the past. His father had always said that he could never really leave it behind until he accepted it.

And Antonio figured Izzy was in the same mix. He had to deal with what he felt for her. Was it just sex? Well, right now of course it was. But it was mixed in with a healthy dose of respect for the woman—the astronaut—she was. She was clearly at the top of the candidate class. It was easy to see from her own ease in the situations that were thrown at them and the way that Dennis, Thor and Ace all treated her.

He could learn from her, and he knew that she had always challenged him to be better. A man who wanted to be with Izzy needed to be at least as good as she was. She had no time for someone who wasn't.

He rubbed the back of his neck, realizing that he had added some extra stress to the next eight weeks.

But it had been so damned pleasurable. As if anything with Izzy could be anything but pleasurable.

"Playboy?"

"Yes, sir?" he answered Thor. He was falling back

into the old military way of addressing his commanding officer. Most of the private space programs used the military structure for their own.

"I asked if you would mind being the leader when the team heads out on the morning ranch chores. You grew up on a ranch, correct?"

"I did. I know more about cattle ranching than I'd like to," he said with a grin. He needed to stop worrying. His brothers would never let him live it down if they knew he had been. He was the middle son in a family of five boys, and his brothers had always pegged him for success. He was carrying more than just his own hopes and dreams with him. He was carrying his family's, as well.

He noticed Izzy watching him. As much as he'd enjoyed their encounter, he knew he had to manage what happened next with her very carefully. He was close to having everything he'd ever wanted...his place in the stars, leadership on a team and, if he were honest, Izzy. She'd always been someone he coveted.

Now he just had to be sure that he didn't screw it up.

Izzy WENT BACK to her room to shower and change for the barbecue. The last thing she wanted to do was think about Antonio or the fact that for the next eight weeks she was going to be spending all of her time with him. She wanted to make it into a test for herself. What better way to see if she was ready for eighteen months in space with him than to spend these next eight weeks honing her skills.

As she ran her hands over her body to wash, she

couldn't help but remember Antonio's and the way he'd held her. There had been so much passion in each of his caresses, it was almost as if he'd imprinted himself on her.

She washed her hair and then stepped out of the shower onto the bath mat. She needed to get him out of her head, but as she toweled off, the memories of their encounter persisted. She remembered every inch of his body and how he'd felt pressed so close to her. She wanted…him.

Again.

Once wasn't going to be enough, and yet it had to be.

One time she could write off as just a bit of fun, but if anything happened between them again, what would the result be? Would her heartbeat accelerate when she thought of him? Would she spend even more time remembering the taste of his kiss and how he'd looked naked? Would she start to lose her chance of getting the payload specialist slot on the first mission?

It was a risk she couldn't take.

She blow-dried her hair and took her time with her makeup. Then she got dressed and realized she had about three hours until she had to be at the lake. She'd already cleaned her room and finished the reading they'd been assigned for the first week of this latest round of training. She got to her feet and walked aimlessly down the hall, looking at the names on each of the doors. She stopped in front of the one marked A. Curzon and rapped on it. She was answered by the sound of a dog barking.

"Who is it?" Antonio called out.

"It's Izzy."

The door opened a smidge and he popped his head out, glancing up and down the hall before he opened it wider and gestured for her to step inside. She did and was greeted by Carly, who seemed to be adjusting to her new quarters. The dog was small and cute.

She was glad she'd put on jeans as she sat on the floor and the little dog jumped onto her crossed legs, curling up between them.

Izzy petted Carly. Her fur was soft to the touch. Izzy had never had a pet growing up. She'd always wanted one, but her life was very demanding, so owning a pet hadn't made much sense.

"I'm happy to see you, but what are you doing here?" Antonio asked.

She petted the little dog one more time and then lifted her to the floor and stood up. "We need to talk."

"That sounds ominous."

"It's not. But I thought it better that we have a few minutes to discuss what happened earlier."

"Fair enough. I need to take Carly for a walk—can we talk then?"

They made their way slowly out of the bunkhouse. The three different bunkhouses surrounded a common park area in a way that looked more like a hotel than a ranch in the middle of Texas Hill Country. The park was green and landscaped, and there were several benches placed under trees that had been dotted around the border.

Izzy rubbed her damp palms on the sides of her jeans, not looking at him. As much as she knew they needed to talk, she was nervous, and for the first time in a good long while she wasn't too sure of what she really wanted.

6

"BOMBSHELL, YOU GOT a minute?"

Izzy glanced over her shoulder and noticed Thor, whose real name was Hemi, standing on the sidewalk. He had a box under one arm and wore a pair of wrap-around shades to block the sun.

"Sure," she said, nodding at Antonio and heading over to see Hemi. "What's up?"

As she got closer she noticed that the box was full of notebooks. Another new training module, no doubt.

"We've had a chance to discuss the teams and they aren't as even skill-wise as we'd like them to be. What are your thoughts on Stephen Miller and Velosi? We're thinking of switching one of them off red team."

"I don't know much about Miller," Izzy asked.

"He's from the EU space program. He is very nearly a double for Velosi in skill set. And, to be honest, you and Curzon are the same way on blue team."

She saw the opportunity and seized it. "It might

make more sense to switch me," Izzy said. Then she wouldn't be in such close proximity to Antonio.

Thor nodded. "Okay. That would work. I will talk to everyone tonight at the get-together at the lake if you are fine with the change."

At an excited bark, they looked around to where Antonio and his little Carly were waiting. Hemi waved them over and dropped to one knee. Antonio let the leash slip from his fingers as the dog ran to greet Hemi ecstatically.

"These two are great friends," Antonio said to her.

"I can see that. Hemi and I were just discussing the fact that the teams aren't as well balanced as they would like. I volunteered to switch with someone on the other team."

"Who?" Antonio asked.

"Stephen Miller. Do you know him?" Hemi asked.

"Yes, we've worked together many times. I've read all of the profiles for the candidates. Are you moving him because of his similarity to Velosi?" Antonio asked.

Hemi nodded, giving Carly one more pet before getting back to his feet. "Why do you ask?"

"Bombshell and Velocity are both NASA and have worked together many times. It might be better to mix things up and separate them," Antonio said. "Just a suggestion."

"Not a bad one," Izzy said. She and Velosi had been together since basic training and they knew each other very well. They worked like cogs in a well-oiled machine.

"Fair point. So would you like to switch with Stephen?" Hemi asked Antonio.

"Sure," Antonio said.

They talked to Hemi for a few more minutes before he left to confirm the change with the others. Izzy wanted to say something light and breezy, but she wasn't really good at light.

She was intense and focused on attaining her goals. She realized she had no real personal skills, and most of the time, that didn't matter. But things had gotten too intimate with Antonio for her to go back to her normal way of freezing him out.

She wanted to do it. Wanted to keep treating him the way she always had, but something had changed inside of her and that was just no longer possible.

"So we should talk," she said at last, sounding lame even to herself.

"Yes. It's a good idea to see where we want to go next," he said.

Izzy chewed her lower lip and then started walking toward the path that led away from the bunkhouses and toward the main ranch house. She heard the jingle of Carly's tags as Antonio followed her. Soon they were walking side by side and she knew she had to say something.

"I don't know," she said at last. "A part of me didn't expect to feel anything other than some sexual relief when we were done."

"I always knew there would be more," he said quietly.

"How did you know that?"

"We have always been like…water and oil—we just don't mix," he said.

She smiled at him. "We don't mix. So why was sex so… Never mind. This is not a conversation I want to have. I think it would be best—"

"Wait a minute. I do want to have that discussion. Sex was good, *querida*. Mind-blowing, even, so now I'm wondering—was it a one-time thing?"

She stopped walking and turned to face him. "Me, too. But we don't have time for a relationship. I don't want to blow my chance at making the inaugural mission and unless you've changed a lot I don't think you do, either. New relationships are distracting and take a lot of care," she said. She'd seen it enough times with her mom as she moved from one man to the next. Always falling passionately in love with them and losing herself in the process.

"They do. And I agree the timing isn't the best, but honestly, Izzy, I don't know how long I'll be able to resist you."

She felt the same. Still, he needed to know that the mission came first for her. Even if that wasn't really what she felt at this moment. "We are going to have to try. What if we were on the mission vehicle or on the space station? We'd have to keep our hands to ourselves. Let's think of this as one more test."

"A test?"

"Yes. Let's see who can last longer," she said. "Who breaks first."

Fear was driving her, making her think of ways to

keep Antonio away from her. "We are going to be in different groups, so we shouldn't see each other that often."

"Except in the gym," he said.

The gym.

She was pretty sure that she'd be doing all of her running outdoors from now on. Except for the AlterG machine. She'd have to be inside for that. And she dreaded it because she knew there was no way she'd be in the gym and not remember Antonio.

AS IF THE emergency bells that had gone off right after they'd made love hadn't been a big enough wake-up call. The dividing of the group into teams and the leveling of those teams had confirmed it. The basic training time was over.

Antonio hadn't come to Cole's Hill, Texas, and the Mick Tanner Training Facility to hook up with Izzy. In fact, he'd planned to stay as far away from her as he could. And calling it "hooking up" wasn't right. It had been more than sex. And he knew that it had been for Izzy, too.

But, as she'd said, they needed to focus. The competition for those remaining team positions on the first mission was fierce. He wanted to make it and he wanted Izzy to make it. He had a few other candidates that he hoped would be on the team as well, but he knew that at this point it was each person for themselves. And there were only three spots left. He respected that. But the roles for those three slots weren't to be filled by just anyone. It was now down to specialty.

He was already distracted having his horse and now a

dog here at the facility with him. And being on a ranch. It brought up all the stuff he'd always been running from. The life that he had never wanted but seemed to fit so easily into. His older brother had laughed his butt off when he'd heard that Antonio had to move out of his high-rise penthouse apartment and back into a bunkhouse on a ranch in the Texas Hill Country.

So of course this thing with Izzy would blow up now. It seemed like it wasn't only the Cronus program director and his commanders who were challenging him. Life itself was throwing up all of his baggage and making him deal with it.

Or at least acknowledge it.

"*Sí*, okay, we will do it your way," he said. "I don't want to jeopardize anything for you or for me."

She gave him one of her rare genuine smiles, full of joy and a touch of innocence that made him want to pull her into his arms and claim her. Promise to protect her from the world and ensure that he was the one who made her smile like that.

But he couldn't do that.

She wouldn't let him even if he'd dared to try.

They were both bold and made their own paths. They could do this. He would do this. He didn't want to break first.

She started walking again. "Let's be friends, though."

Friends.

Yeah, that was going to help him. Like getting to know the woman who was setting his senses on fire was going to help him keep her at arm's length.

"I don't know if that's a good idea," he said.

She pushed her sunglasses up on her head, stirring the hair she had pulled back into a ponytail and causing a strand to fall forward. He reached out and tucked it back behind her ear, and a shiver of heat ran down his spine. Unless he figured out a way to get his lust under control, he was doomed.

The funny thing about his call sign was that he didn't have a rapacious appetite for women. Sure, he'd always enjoyed them. Liked talking to them, touching them, listening to them. And that had drawn them to him over the years.

Now he was this close to the one woman whose story he really wanted to hear, and he felt it would be dangerous to hear it. Plus, he didn't want to go back to the way things had been, when they'd only traded barbs.

"Okay, friends," he said.

"Are you sure?" she asked. "We were friends those first few weeks at basic training."

"Yes, we were. You were very kind to me," he said.

"You noticed me as a person and not just an hourglass figure with a nice rack," she said. "That made you easy to be nice to."

He'd forgotten how tough some of the other men had been to her and how sweet she really had seemed those first few weeks, before she'd had to toughen up and prove to everyone in their training group that she was the baddest thing since Rambo.

"So, friend, what do you want to talk about?"

"Ranching," she said. "Do you have any cowboy tips? I think I mentioned I do not really like being on a ranch."

He started laughing. "Me, neither. My brothers have been ribbing me about the fact that the very thing I left Argentina to avoid is now part of my daily routine again."

"So you're not any good at it?" she asked. "I've been spending my Sundays off taking horseback riding lessons on a neighboring ranch to improve my skills."

Of course she was. Izzy always made sure she did whatever was necessary to succeed. And he had to do the same.

"Actually, I'm really good at it," he admitted. "But nothing could really compete with the thought of being up there in the stars. Racing toward a planet that no other person has been on."

"Same," she said. "I think we are going to be very good friends."

GOOD FRIENDS. SHE could do it. It made a sort of sense, since she wasn't going to be able to just ignore him. She'd been friends with guys before… Velosi and Hemi sprang to mind.

"How many brothers do you have?" she asked as they walked around the man-made lake. There was a path that was bordered with stones and gaslights. Over by the dock she saw a few of the ranch hands swimming. It was April in Texas, which meant it was hot. She'd grown up in Vegas so she was used to the heat.

"Four. I'm smack in the middle," Antonio said. "What about you?"

"Only child," she said.

"Did you ever wish for a sibling?" he asked.

"No." Maybe because her mom had had several marriages when Izzy was growing up, and some of the men had kids from previous marriages. She'd always found that she was most comfortable by herself with her nose in a book. "Did you ever wish to be an only child?" she asked.

He shook his head. "I can't imagine life without my brothers. We are very close. Sometimes they're a pain in the ass, but when I need them they are always there for me."

That was one thing she didn't have. Her mom was always there for her, but it was just the two of them. Her mom had stopped with the serial marriages around the time Izzy turned eighteen and had spent the last ten years on her own. Discovering herself, as she liked to put it.

"Before I came out here the closest I'd been to a cowboy, aside from Ace, was at the Professional Bull Riders championship every year in Vegas. But that's got some flash. This is just hard work," she said. "Was that why you didn't want to be a cowboy?"

He shook his head as they rounded the lake and started up the path that led back to the bunkhouses. "If it was, I didn't choose wisely. Being an astronaut is a lot of hard work, as you know."

"What did draw you to the program?"

"Just always spent a lot of time looking up at the stars, wondering if there was life out there."

"Do you think there is?" she asked. "I mean, when I was on the ISS, I thought about encountering something else. Probably just a leftover fantasy from my teen years."

"Me, too. It would be ignorant to think we're the only beings in the universe."

"I agree. Some of my friends from high school asked me if I wanted to meet an alien. As if that was why I wanted to be an astronaut," she said.

He nodded. "I think most people are both hoping there is something else out there and afraid of what it might be. Probably because of Hollywood versions of aliens."

Izzy wasn't too sure. She knew logically there had to be someone else out there, but a part of her—the part that didn't really like change—wasn't too keen on finding another species. The Earth inhabitants might not be the only ones who were trying to get to a planet like Mars. Or maybe even to Mars.

"Maybe," she conceded.

"Want to hear something funny?" he asked.

"Sure."

"My oldest brother, Salvatore, always warns me about hostile aliens. He's pretty sure that anyone we meet will be scared and it might trigger a confrontation."

She laughed, as she suspected he was speaking more about her than about aliens. "When I was cleared for my first mission I started having nightmares where I was on the spaceship from *Aliens*. And I couldn't run. You know how we sleep up there, all strapped in and everything. I didn't sleep for the first three days as I got used to it, and then my body just forced the issue," she said. She could still remember the cold fear in her stomach as she'd thought of encountering something malevolent in space.

"Well, you don't have to worry about that. Cronus is going to be our first successful foray beyond our orbit and I think we are going to discover many beautiful things out there," Antonio said.

He made it easy to believe. Just by spending time with him, she was already uncovering things that she'd never thought of before. A part of her wished that she'd gotten to know him sooner, but she knew she might not be here if she had. Something about Antonio made her feel she could easily fall in love with him.

And if she were anything like her mom, chances were she would have put his career on the fast track and her own on the back burner.

They parted ways at the bunkhouse and, as she watched him walk away, Izzy made up her mind to keep her distance from Antonio. She couldn't be just friends with him, because she knew she wanted so much more than friendship. She'd freeze him out. It might hurt to cut him off, but better to deal with that loss now than to lose something bigger—like her chance at the Cronus mission.

7

ANTONIO AND HIS team were gelling pretty well. He looked forward to the new challenges that each day brought, but if he were honest he had to admit that he also missed Izzy. The sessions were intense, though, and there really wasn't time for any fraternization. No chance to tempt her away from keeping things platonic.

But tonight they were all going into town to celebrate the engagement of Thor and Jessie Odell. Jessie, an extreme survival expert, was the daughter of famous nature documentary makers. She'd grown up on different nature shows on TV that had been broadcast all over the world. He'd had classes with Jessie, and it had taken only one lesson before he'd realized that she wasn't a "celebrity" but someone who actually knew her stuff.

Because everyone at the facility and the ranch was attending the party, they'd rented a hotel ballroom in the Five Families area of Cole's Hill—a posh neighborhood with mansion-size houses and a championship golf course. Six Hummer limos would transport everyone to and from the party.

Antonio had taken Carly for a walk, played with her and then crated her for her evening in. He had taken care with his clothing, but then he always did. His father said that clothes weren't enough to make a woman fall in love, but heads turned more quickly for someone who looked like he'd taken time with his appearance.

Hennessy and Meredith were already in the limo when he climbed in. They were both on his team and were specialists with backgrounds in theoretical physics. They were deep in a very technical conversation about potential anomalies the teams might encounter.

The scent of wildflowers and cinnamon preceded Izzy as she climbed into the limo. She wore a light summer dress that was loose and flowy around her waist and hips, and skimmed the top of her thighs. Their eyes met and he felt a flash of heat go through him. He'd missed her.

He might have spent the last week seeing her in his dreams, but those dreams paled with the reality of her. Her skin seemed creamier than he remembered, her lips lusher, her limbs longer and her smile sweeter.

"Hey, you," she said, taking a seat next to him.

"Hey. How's it been going?"

"Not too bad. I haven't suddenly decided that I want to be a cowgirl, I'll tell you that."

He laughed. "That's probably a good thing."

"Agreed. How's the simulator?" she asked. "I'm dying to start working the large maneuvering arm. I've been playing with the program on my laptop, but it's not the same as using the actual device."

He loved that they shared an engineering background. "It's good, very similar to the old shuttle payload crane. I have notes on some changes I'd like to see made—I'll be interested to know what you think," he said.

"I can't wait. Next week I'll be in there," she said, then changed the subject. "You look nice tonight."

"As do you," he said.

"After days of wearing jeans and boots and being sweaty from riding fence or moving cattle from one pasture to another... I can't wait to be back in my Cronus golf shirt and khakis and focusing on moving different sections of the way station into position. Who else has been operating the equipment?"

They discussed the other candidates who were payload specialists as the limo filled up and then it was time to go. Someone turned on the radio, and everyone groaned as Elton John's "Rocket Man" played.

"I used to love this song," Izzy said. "Mom took me to see Elton John in Vegas one time. He was really good."

"It's okay. I prefer 'Space Oddity,'" Antonio said. "My second-oldest brother plays classical Spanish guitar and always plays it for me when I'm home," he said.

He missed his brothers. He was used to being away from them, but usually had some contact. Here at the training facility, they were being acclimated to long absences from their family and friends, with only weekly emails allowed, and no phone or video calls.

But Carlos had sent him a digital file of his music and whenever Antonio missed home, he played it.

"As far as 'space' songs are concerned, I'm a big fan of 'Satellite' by Dave Matthews Band," Izzy said.

"That's a good one," Antonio said. The radio cut out while someone plugged in an iPod, and then "Starboy" by The Weeknd featuring Daft Punk started playing and everyone went wild, clapping and singing along.

"Love this song," Izzy said.

He nodded, feeling oddly melancholy. She was doing the friend thing. Making it seem that they had never seen each other naked. And he saw how pale an imitation it was from what they could have.

He resented it.

He knew that part of what he felt stemmed directly from the fact that she looked so damned good tonight and he wanted her.

He hated having to deny himself Izzy.

For a few brief moments when they'd been in each other's arms, he'd caught a tiny glimpse of what could be and he craved it.

He wanted her. He needed her. And right now he knew only one thing with totally certainty—to hell with being friends.

Izzy spent the night drinking mocktails and dancing with everyone in the Cronus candidate program except Antonio.

He was funny and smart and quick-witted. Not a lot of people checked so many boxes for her. But of course he did. He always had, she realized, which was precisely why she'd tried to avoid him.

She groaned.

"You okay?"

Meredith Korman was one of the other women in the candidate program. Her call sign was Brainiac. She was smart—like scary intelligent. She was also a little on the shy side but very nice.

"Yes. Just struggling with something."

"Playboy?" Meredith asked.

"What? Is it that obvious?" Izzy asked her friend, taking another sip of the nonalcoholic mojito and wishing it were the real thing.

"Not really. It's just I saw the two of you in the limo. Don't take this the wrong way, but you were trying hard to be all cool and it looked…well, painful," Meredith said.

"Well, nuts."

Meredith laughed. "I doubt anyone else noticed."

"Except Antonio," Izzy muttered.

"Probably. That man doesn't miss much. So do you want to talk about it?"

She could use someone to talk to, someone who could reinforce she'd made the right decision when she'd shut Antonio down. "Unless you know some way to make me magically stop wanting him…" Izzy said.

Meredith laughed again. "I bet I could make a million dollars if I came up with some sort of synthetic spray or pill that could make that happen."

"You could," Izzy said. For the first time in her life she actually understood why her mother had been in so many relationships. This feeling…it wasn't love because it wasn't that deep, but it was affection. A feeling of butterflies in her stomach whenever she looked at him or thought about him. A little bit of obsession. She wanted to groan again but stopped herself.

"If it makes you feel any better, he does look at you when you aren't paying attention," Meredith said. "I think whatever is going on between the two of you is mutual."

"That doesn't make it any easier. You'd think with training, my mind and body would be exhausted every day—and they are—but also there are moments when I'm wide-awake in the middle of the night and can only think about him," Izzy said. "Sorry to be rambling on about it."

"I did invite you to," Meredith said.

"Thank you for that. How are you finding the program?" Izzy asked, wanting to turn the topic from her personal life.

"I love it. I'm not really looking forward to having to do the ranching part. The simulator is everything I'd hoped it would be. My section is isolated from the others and the work is so satisfying. I really am excited to be on the project."

Izzy was a little concerned that Meredith liked being alone. That might raise a problem down the road if she were selected for a mission. The teams all had to function together.

"I'm glad to hear that."

"Thanks," Meredith said. "I think the first limo is heading back soon. I'm going to be in it. You coming?"

Izzy shook her head. She wasn't ready to leave yet. Meredith got up and left, and Izzy decided it was time to stop ignoring Antonio. She had to figure out what exactly was going on between them.

He was by far the handsomest man in the room. For someone with his reputation, he was not living up to it tonight. He'd spent most of the time at one of the high bar tables talking to Ace and Dennis.

She walked over to the men and they all looked up and smiled at her, Antonio rose from his chair and held it out to her. "Please join us."

"We were watching everyone mix and trying to decide if we should discourage the candidates from…" Dennis trailed off.

"Hooking up?" she suggested.

"Well, yes," he said, a little chagrined. "No one has really made a decision on whether or not couples would be sent on the Cronus mission and so far we haven't had an astronaut couple apply. But watching the group tonight made it clear we might to have to deal with that at some point."

Izzy felt a shiver run down her spine as Antonio glanced at her. They had to be careful. Neither of them wanted to do anything that would hurt their chances of making the team, but if Dennis decided against couples…

"Luckily that's not an issue," Izzy said.

Molly arrived, and Dennis excused himself so Molly and Ace could dance. Antonio looked over at Izzy and her earlier resolve came back.

She held out her hand to him. "Wanna dance?"

HEMI'S BROTHER MANU, the former defensive end for an NFL team and now a special teams coach for the NFL, was the deejay for the evening. He kept the music lively and the dance floor full by playing a blend of modern country and Top 40 hits combined with perennial dance favorites. He also used the time between songs to share stories of Hemi that kept the candidates and ranch hands laughing. Most of them saw Thor only as a serious astronaut.

He took Izzy's hand and followed her to the dance floor as Manu played "Cake by the Ocean" by DNCE. Izzy danced the way she did everything else, with ease and grace. He watched her, for once not having to hide his interest.

Talking to Ace and Dennis had brought home the fact that he might have to choose: Izzy or the Cronus mission. Which made their decision to be only friends all the more important. That wasn't helping to calm the blood flowing heavily through his veins.

He watched her mouth as she sang along to the song. Wanted to kiss her again, remembered how her lips had felt under his and wondered why he had ever thought that once would be enough. Wondered if he could have her one more time and still maintain a little of his sanity.

He doubted it.

Though not having her wasn't exactly helping his sanity, either.

He caught her hand as the music changed to "Closer" by The Chainsmokers, and he pulled her into his body, swaying along with the music. She wrapped her arms around his neck and their eyes met.

He saw the same desire, the same pent-up longing and confusion in her eyes that he felt deep in his soul. He rested his forehead against hers and closed his eyes, but that made the keen longing worse.

Her perfume was subtle but distinctive and he remembered how it had lingered on his skin after they'd made love the first time. Her body was warm and curvy, pressing into his as they moved, and he suddenly didn't care about anything but Izzy.

He moved them around the dance floor to a corner of the room hidden from view. He put one hand on her hip and the other on the wall behind them.

"What are you doing, Antonio?" she asked.

"Taking a chance that you are as unhappy with the 'just friends' thing as I am," he said, mere inches of space between them.

"I am," she whispered. "I'm so torn right now. I can't stop thinking about you, Playboy. I can't figure out if being lovers would fix the problem."

"It can't hurt," he said. He wasn't concerned that she'd called him by his call sign because the old edge to her tone was gone.

"I hope you're right," she said, looking up into his eyes.

He was taking a risk. Hell, so was she. Dennis and Ace were watching them all and looking for reasons to bench candidates to make the pool smaller and their decision easier. But he knew that denying himself Izzy wasn't helping his chances.

She distracted him and he couldn't let her continue to do so.

He took her hand loosely in his and led her out of the ballroom at the historic Grand Hotel located on Main Street and led her through the lobby to the front desk.

"Are there any rooms available for tonight?" he asked the desk clerk.

Izzy squeezed his hand as the clerk handed them a key. Antonio had the presence of mind to ask for a late checkout before he took Izzy's hand in his.

She matched him step for step and he had a flash of the two of them in their space suits walking up the gangplank to the rocket together. He wanted that to be true, wanted her in his bed, in his life and in space with him. But for tonight only one of those things mattered. When they turned away from the open balcony area and down the private corridor that led to their room, she tugged him to a stop. Wrapping her arms around him, she went up on tiptoe and kissed him with all the passion he'd seen in her the last time they'd been intimate.

This time was better. He knew what she liked and angled his head to deepen the kiss. Her tongue slid over his and she sucked his deeper into her mouth. He put his hands on her hips and drew her into the cradle of his thighs.

For the longest time he let the kiss deepen. She rubbed her center over his growing erection and finally he lifted his head and looked down into her heart-shaped face. Her skin was flushed and rosy, her lips full and glistening. She watched him with a surety that made him want to toss her over his shoulder and run to the room.

But he settled for taking her hand in his and leading her there.

8

"I LEFT MY purse and phone downstairs," Izzy said as they walked into their suite.

"I'll get them…after," he said. His voice was guttural.

Desire seemed to have stripped away the level of sophistication and civility that Antonio always wore like a mantle. A part of her had resented it because it was the kind of attitude that couldn't be aped or learned. It came from being born with money and growing up secure.

But she'd shaken him to his core. She did like that.

Licking her suddenly dry lips, she took him by his tie and exerted a slight pressure, not enough to hurt him but enough to let him know she wanted him to follow her.

He gave her a cocky half grin, raised one eyebrow and did as she commanded. She drew him to the small sitting area and pushed him down into a padded armchair. He spread his legs wide and put his hands on the arms of the chair.

She took a step back and then slowly bent forward,

knowing she was giving him a view down her bodice as she undid the buckle to her left sandal first and then her right. She stood back up slowly, and their eyes met.

She felt the heat in his gaze as he watched her. Moving deliberately, she stepped out of her shoes, then slowly lifted the hem of her dress, drawing the fabric up her legs. She hadn't worn any hose on this hot May evening and the soft cotton-blend fabric felt good against her skin. She reached under her dress and pulled off her underwear, kicking it to the side, next to her shoes.

He sat up straighter in the chair and beckoned her forward with the crook of one long finger.

She shook her head and arched her eyebrow at him. "You're not ready for me yet."

"Oh, I'm ready," he promised her.

"Show me," she said.

He slowly undid his belt, drawing it from around his waist and letting it snap when it was free. A shiver of anticipation went down her spine. Her breasts felt fuller and her nipples tightened as he undid his pants, shifting on the chair until he was able to free his cock and balls.

His erection was thick and long, and he stroked himself as he watched her.

"Satisfied?"

"Not yet, but I think I will be," she said. She took a step toward him, only stopping when her skirt brushed the fabric of his trousers.

He shifted forward quickly and caught her unawares, lifting her off her feet and settling her so she straddled him. The fabric of her dress bunched between their bodies as he wrapped his hand around the back of her neck.

His fingers fanned out along the side of her face, strok-ing her cheek and then fondling her earlobe. A shudder of need went through her and she canted her mouth to-ward his, but he turned away. She felt the bristle of his beard against her lips and it sent another shiver down her spine.

Rubbing his thumb over her bottom lip made it tingle and she reached up, taking his wrist in her hand. She found his mouth with hers, their tongues tangling. She felt his fingers feather-light against that spot at the base of her spine. Trembling with need, she tried to deepen the kiss, but Antonio was firmly in control, no matter that she was in the dominant position. He wasn't rush-ing things.

She wanted to force him to move faster, yet at the same time she enjoyed the delicate torture of his pro-longed kisses and caresses. His breath tasted of mint and passion. After a life spent following procedure and denying herself, she knew this was something worth breaking the rules for.

She'd been in Cole's Hill—the neighboring town to the Bar T ranch and the training facility—and Izzy had been there for a long time, being tested, showing her expertise and facing every challenge thrown at her by NASA and the Cronus mission commander and di-rector. Yet she was no closer to getting anything she wanted. After a lifetime of trying not to be her mom, refusing to make bad choices when it came to men, she didn't care anymore.

The way Antonio moved his tongue over her bottom lip was sending pulses straight to her core. His hands

creasing the pace of her strokes. His hips canted forward and his tongue plunged deeper into her mouth as his hand shifted on her breast and she felt her dress being drawn up. They broke the kiss long enough for him to pull it off and toss it aside. All she wore now was a tiny bandeau-type strapless bra.

He arched an eyebrow at her as he slowly peeled it up and over her head. Then he put both hands on her breasts, cupping them, pushing them together as he leaned in and his breath brushed over her cleavage. He dropped nibbling kisses along the full globes and then bit her at the base of her left breast.

"Ouch."

"Sorry, *querida*," he said. "I wanted to leave my mark on you so when we go back to real life you will know this really happened."

She shifted around and leaned down and bit him above his left nipple with the same force. Then she soothed the area with her tongue and sucked hard on his skin, and when she lifted her head she knew he'd have a love bite to remember her.

"Tit for tat? Isn't that what you Americans say?"

"I don't know, but I'm all about keeping the playing field level," Izzy said. Finally she pulled his shirts over his head, getting him fully naked. It was then that she noticed the gold medallion he wore. She lifted it up. It was the size of a quarter and hot from being pressed against his skin. She leaned over and kissed the spot on his chest where it had lain and then dropped it back down.

Putting her hands on his shoulders, she shifted until

she felt the tip of him at her entrance, and this time he didn't stop her. Instead, he put his hands on her hips and urged her down. She had to move slowly to accommodate his size. But soon he was fully seated inside her and she felt those delicious shivers again, spreading out from where they were joined. She wanted to move, but he held her still with his hands as he lowered his head and took one nipple in his mouth. He held it lightly between his teeth and twirled his tongue around it. She was desperate to move, and she put her hand against his neck, urging his head back with her thumb.

She leaned forward, her mouth open as she rubbed her lips over his neck and tightened her internal muscles around him. He groaned and his tongue snaked out to touch hers. She sucked it into her mouth and shifted again, and this time he let her move. She moved up on his length until he was almost out of her body and then slowly slid back down him again. She moved her mouth over his, leaving wet kisses all along his jawline as she moved against him, riding him slowly. Letting the storm within her build up. She held herself in check, taking him slowly because, now that he was inside her again, she knew she didn't want to let this moment end. Didn't want to chance losing him.

But he felt so damned good. He put his hands on her hips, driving up into her. Their joining was frantic, both of them becoming more urgent with each stroke. His mouth took control of hers and she felt his hands in her hair. His other hand found her hip and gripped it hard. His tongue thrust into her mouth as his hips thrust into her body, pushing her more quickly toward her climax. She held on to him, her tongue tangling with his, her body searching for release. Then he tore his mouth from hers and buried his head in the crook of her neck as he groaned and she felt him spilling himself into her.

His release triggered her own, and she closed her eyes tightly as her orgasm rocked through her. Antonio kept thrusting into her, the pace slowing until she collapsed against him, resting her head on his shoulder as he swept his hands up and down her back.

The caresses on her back grew lighter and then he placed his hand under her chin and lifted her head so that their eyes met.

"Each time we are together I tell myself no woman can make me feel as good as you do, and each time I am wrong," he said.

He was exactly what she needed—and exactly what she was afraid of.

There was a very good chance that Antonio had already broken something at her core. That glass wall she'd used to keep everyone away so she could focus on one thing—the space program.

She wanted to feel regret or anger, but she didn't. How could she when he held her so tenderly?

He withdrew from her and stood up, holding her in his arms. She felt him step out of his trousers, which had pooled at his ankles. He carried her into the bathroom, where she saw a large garden tub and intimate lighting just over it. He set her on the counter as he washed up.

"I believe I need to go and fetch your phone and purse, and I'm going to ask Ace to look in on Carly.

Why don't you run a bath and I'll be right back?" he suggested.

She nodded and hopped off the counter to fiddle with the taps on the tub while she heard him dressing.

"I'll be right back," he promised again, and came to kiss her before letting himself out of their suite.

She felt a pang as he left. In a small way, it mirrored the reality of their lives. They were going to be apart more than they were together. Even if the Cronus mission accepted couples, they were a long way from that stage. They were still feeling their way around things. Sex was hot, but the friend thing…well, that was hot and cold.

She thought about putting her dress on and sneaking back down to the limos, going back to her room at the bunkhouse and denying this had happened.

But she'd never run from the hard things in her life and she wasn't about to now. Antonio was changing her. Making her care for him.

Damn. She couldn't even make herself say *love*. But it wasn't love. Not yet. And if she was careful, it never would be.

She wanted Cronus. But for now she wanted Antonio, too. And if she put her mind to it, she could have both. She just had to be willing to let him go when the time came.

She turned her attention back to the bath, carefully monitoring the temperature and adding in salts that the hotel had so thoughtfully provided along with some high-end bubble bath that smelled like lavender. She put the bath mat on the floor, adjusted the lighting, then climbed into the tub just as the door to the suite opened again.

"I'm back."

"I'm glad," she said. She wasn't going to try to put up walls to keep him out tonight. She was going to give herself this time with Antonio. Soon enough they would be facing the rigors of training.

He stood in the doorway with her purse and phone and another bag in his other hand. "I picked us up some snacks for later."

She nodded but said nothing as he went into the other room. She watched him go and this time it didn't hurt. She'd like to think that was because she'd made the decision to let him go and not because she knew he'd be coming right back.

9

ANTONIO TOOK OFF his dress shirt and trousers and went back into the bathroom wearing only his boxers and carrying one of his favorite books. He'd seen it in the lobby gift store when he'd gone back for Izzy's stuff. He poured two glasses of sparkling water—they were both in training and alcohol wasn't something that either of them drank.

The conversation he'd overheard between Ace and Dennis should have made him leave her alone tonight. They'd been discussing the fact that couples shouldn't be sent to space. They were worried that some of the candidates might hook up, and they felt couples who had just gotten together over the course of training should definitely not be chosen for a mission together.

Should he tell Izzy?

He stood in the doorway for a few moments unobserved and just watched her. She made his pulse race. Hell, just thinking about her unnerved him. But watching her.

Damn.

He'd just had her and he wanted her again. He knew that was the ticking clock in his head driving him to make the most of these quiet moments when they could almost forget about the future and the mission.

He knew astronauts who were married, who had normal lives and spouses who kept the home fires burning, but that had never been on his radar. He had been a loner for as long as he could remember…and now there was Izzy. His fellow traveler on a journey that would hopefully take them away from their home. Which was why he'd bought this book. His favorite book, and the gift shop had even had a Spanish copy, an advantage of being based in Texas.

He cleared his throat.

There was a melancholy air about her, and he hoped she wasn't thinking too much about tomorrow and the roles they'd have to go back into.

"May I join you?" he asked.

She lifted her arm and a cascade of water droplets fell into the tub and onto the floor as she waved for him to enter. "I've never shared a tub with anyone."

"That's okay. I thought I'd just keep you company and maybe read to you," he said.

"Of course," she said. She'd tucked her hair behind her ears, and she tipped her head from where it was pillowed on a folded-up towel, and looked back at him. "What book?"

"Le Petit Prince," he said, putting a towel on the tile next to the tub. "It's in Spanish, I hope you don't mind. This is my favorite book."

She shook her head. "I love it, too. I am familiar enough with the story that my high school Spanish should be enough."

He sat down on the towel and opened the book, re-membering his mom reading it to him when he was a boy. This book had always soothed the darkness inside. The longings, resentment and other emotions that he didn't like to deal with.

He started reading. The words fell easily from his mouth and he forgot about the future and the choices he was going to have to make. Izzy or Cronus, but not both. That was what Dennis and Ace had been hinting at. Hooking up with other candidates wasn't a good idea.

Still, as he read, he remembered always thinking as a child that he was like the Little Prince. Funny, his career choice made it more likely that he was going to be the Prince.

He paused to look at Izzy, who had turned on her side to watch him. The water had to be cooling and he saw that her shoulder and left breast were visible and had gooseflesh.

"You're cold. I'm sorry. I should have noticed ear-lier," he said, putting the book aside and standing to get her a towel.

"I didn't notice. You have a lovely voice, Antonio. I could have listened to you until the water turned to ice," she said, rising and stepping delicately onto the bath mat. He handed her the towel.

"I'm happy to keep reading to you in bed," he said.

"I'd like that. I wish I had a nightshirt," she said.

"You can sleep in my T-shirt."

"Your fantasy?"

"Part of it," he said, not elaborating. It wasn't that he didn't trust her with his dreams and desires—it was simply that the more he shared with her, the tighter the intimate bond between them grew. He was so afraid that there was going to come a time when he'd forget where he ended and she began.

He led the way back into the main living area of the suite and then through the door that led to the bedroom. He went to his clothing, which he'd draped over one of the chairs near the small table, and held his T-shirt out to her.

But his breath caught in his chest as he saw her leaning over the dresser and looking in the mirror. At first her curvy, naked body captured his gaze, and then as he skimmed up her frame, their eyes met in the mirror. She'd been watching him watch her.

They were both so afraid to risk anything with each other. Perhaps there was a reason they'd let their competitive streaks keep them apart all these years.

But as she turned and walked to him, taking the shirt from his hand and pulling it on, he couldn't for the life of him believe that it mattered.

Instead, he followed her to the bed, and after a few minutes they were situated with pillows behind his back and her cuddled against his side. "What time do you have to be back at the facility?" he asked.

"I have the morning free," she said. "So noon. You?"

"Same. I'm doing the evening chores." He reached for his phone and set the alarm.

"What shall we do now?" he asked.

"Would you mind reading to me some more?" she asked.

He tightened his arm around her and then reached for the book. He found the page and read until Izzy drifted to sleep. And he thought to himself that, like the Little Prince, if he was ever stranded on another world he would do anything in his power to get back to Izzy.

Izzy woke with a start. She had a moment's disorientation as her heart raced and she wondered where the hell she was. Then she knew. Cole's Hill. She was at the historic Grand Hotel.

In a suite.

With Antonio.

She looked over her shoulder and saw his broad back. They were pressed back-to-back with each other. She'd fallen asleep to the sound of his voice reading to her in Spanish. It was a memory that she was going to treasure for a long time.

Her mouth felt dry so she got out of bed, careful not to disturb him, and went into the other room. Finding a bottle of water in the minibar, she drank it in two long gulps. She walked to the window that overlooked the back parking lot and the sky.

One of the things she loved about Texas was how big the sky was here. Not Montana big, but still, when she looked up at it at night, she could get lost searching for constellations and planets. Tonight was no different.

She wanted to be like the prince in the story, be able to shed the shell that was her past and her fears of being like her mom. It didn't matter that earlier she'd thought she'd put that ghost to rest. She hadn't.

She doubted she ever would.

There was no way to outrun the past; she'd known that for a long time. There were times when her rebel streak got the best of her and she just had to give in to the things she craved.

Antonio.

There hadn't been a lot of men in her life who had affected her the way he did. She wasn't going to deny that he had a powerful pull on her, much like the moon did on the oceans. She just wasn't sure if they were coming into a season where he was going to turn her into an out-of-control hurricane.

There was a chance… Hell, it was more than a chance—it was a definite possibility. But not tonight.

As she watched the moon, she realized that she wasn't ready for the night to end. Tomorrow, when they showed up at the bunkhouse in yesterday's clothes, how would they explain themselves? For that matter, how were they even going to get back?

It wasn't like there was a huge cab service in Cole's Hill, and calling Hemi or Ace and asking for a ride wasn't high on her list of things she wanted to do. But she supposed she'd have to. Being a grown-ass woman meant owning up to her actions. She knew that. Always had.

But right now, she wanted to hide. To stay here in this room with Antonio and pretend nothing else existed.

She heard his footsteps a few moments before he put his arms around her and drew her back against his body.

"You okay?" he asked.

She nodded. "Just staring up at the night sky and thinking."

"Good thoughts?" His arms around her comforted her from the drama she was creating in her head. All her life she thought she'd been at war with herself. Proud of how hard her mom worked, yet at the same determined not to be swayed by men the way her mom had been.

"Yeah."

He made a tsking sound and turned her in his arms to face him.

"Let's don't lie to each other," he said. "I know that we have enough obstacles to this being a strong relationship already."

"I wasn't lying to you. They are good thoughts. I remembered the deep rumble of your voice as I went to sleep and now I'm searching the sky for the Little Prince's home planet…good, happy thoughts," she said. But even to her own ears she sounded a little defensive.

She couldn't help it. She had worked herself into the kind of state she usually needed the gym for. Work out to get rid of the energy and force herself to stop thinking.

"*Querida*, I promise you that I will not judge," he said.

She just arched one eyebrow at him. "Why would you be judging me?"

"I don't know. What are you thinking about?" he asked her.

"That this is a mistake. That sleeping with you once

was okay because I wrote it off as curiosity, but doing it again—this is becoming a habit."

"Habit?"

"No judging, right?"

He put his hands up and stepped away from her. She knew she should have kept her mouth shut, but something about Antonio made her want to tell him everything.

Where Antonio was concerned, she wasn't the ice queen she knew the men called her behind her back, and that should bother her more than it did.

But a part of her was relieved to be herself. Even if it was her not-perfect stuff. She was real with him and she liked it.

More than she wanted to.

The problem was that she didn't know how to be herself *and* be successful. It scared her—it also excited her.

NOT JUDGING WASN'T really hard for him. For as long as he could remember he'd been the different one, the odd one. He was lucky to have grown up in a family that supported him and urged him to follow his dreams. That had made it easier for him to push aside the opinions of others.

But this wasn't about him. It was about Izzy.

"Of course," he said.

She nibbled on her lower lip and then turned away from the window wearing only his T-shirt. He was honest enough to admit he was distracted. She wasn't tall, but her limbs seemed long, her legs endless and her arms so slim and graceful. Her waist was tiny, not that he could see it with his shirt draped over her.

She perched on the arm of the love seat and crossed one leg over the other, swinging her foot. He groaned as he thought about putting his hands on her thighs and parting her legs.

He wanted her.

Not really a big surprise.

But she needed to talk.

When his father gave him and his brothers the man-woman talk, part of his advice had been to listen to women. His papa had been adamant that there was more to sex than just the physical act. And Antonio knew he needed to be the man he'd always thought he was, and not a raging bundle of hormones. But it was damned hard.

"Izzy?"

"It's just every time I think of how to say it, the words sound dumb in my head. I mean, I know what I want to say and it makes sense in my mind, but if I say it out loud…"

He knew exactly what she meant. "Try thinking in one language and having to speak in another, and then add in worrying about how you might sound."

"I forgot about that. You speak English so well. It doesn't seem to really affect you. Plus, you're smart."

"So are you," he reminded her. "What is it that you want to say and are struggling with?"

She shrugged, and he closed the gap between them to sit on the coffee table near her.

"Whisper it. I'm close enough to hear it."

She slid off the arm of the couch and onto the seat. Dropping her hands on her knees, she scooted closer.

"I feel like an idiot."

"Everyone knows you aren't one," he said.

"With you... I don't feel pressured to be what everyone else needs me to be. I can be myself and that's very freeing. Does that make sense?"

He shook his head. Izzy was one of the strongest, most dominant people he knew, man or woman. "Are you sure you aren't being something else with me? Not that we've even had a chance to explore who we are. It's hard to be a couple when we are trying to avoid each other."

"Fair enough," she said. "I guess that with you I *want* to be my authentic self. Not the woman I always am at work. Even in personal relationships, I tend to keep it all about the physical, which kind of puts a stale date on the relationship. But with you, that doesn't work," she admitted.

He took her hands and turned them over in his, mainly to distract himself because even though her words thrilled him, he didn't want to mean that much to her. It would be easier for him if this was purely physical for both of them. That way they could have fun but put their careers first.

He felt a lot of pressure. Everyone was watching him and the other candidates from Space Now to see how the private company performed, so they needed to be doing it better and cleaner than everyone else.

"It doesn't work for me, either," he said at last. "I sort of wished it would."

She laughed. "Me, too. Would be easier to hook up and walk away, but I can't. I think about you all the time and I wonder… I wonder if we do this dating thing, if that will be enough to bring us back to center. Maybe if we tried seeing each other in the off time we'd get bored with each other," she said.

"Maybe." He tried to sound noncommittal, then thought about how honest she'd been with him. He needed to be straight with her, as well. "Izzy. Before you joined us earlier, Dennis and Ace both were very frank in their discussions about the candidates and fraternizing."

"So? Ace knows me and he knows you, too. We're both very good at our jobs," she said. "Do they think it will affect us?"

"It's not us specifically. To be fair, they were talking in generalities. It's just that you know I'm not from NASA, and I don't want to risk it all—"

"For me."

When she put it that way he felt like a douche bag. "No. Not that. What I mean is, I feel the scrutiny that the Space Now candidates are under, and I just don't want to give Ace and Dennis an excuse to mark me down."

She nodded. "So…?"

"We do need to sort this out. How would you feel about talking to Ace tomorrow, telling him we'd like to date and have no idea where it's going to go. We can tell him we'll see if it affects our training and our work."

She sat back and watched him for a long time, and he wondered if he'd been too honest with her.

"I think it's a good idea. Because avoiding each other

has sucked. Plus, I'm not sure that I'll be able to just shut you out of my life," she admitted.

"Me, neither," he agreed.

He scooped her up in his arms and carried her back to bed, where he made love to her and pretended that everything was resolved. But he knew that it hadn't been.

10

Izzy CALLED DOWN to the front desk and arranged for a rental car while Antonio was in the shower. She also asked them to send up some clothes from the gift store in their sizes and gave them her credit card number to pay for everything.

She knocked on the bathroom door and poked her head inside. "How does room service sound for breakfast?"

"Perfect," Antonio said.

"I'm running downstairs to get the keys to the car I rented. I'll be right back."

She let herself out of the room and went downstairs, noticing that Velosi and his wife were having breakfast in the restaurant just off the lobby.

They didn't need to hide anything. They didn't need to worry their romance would keep Velosi from space. Margaret had flown in from Florida for the weekend and the two of them were sitting side by side in a booth, their heads close together as they talked.

She sighed as she watched them. Velosi had been dating Margaret when Izzy had first met him, and they were one of those couples that seemed absolutely perfect together. She knew a lot of that was due to the fact that they had different roles in the relationship. Margaret was the daughter of a Marine Corps general and was used to having the male in the household gone for long stints of time.

How could she and Antonio make this work? They were both the one who was always leaving. Neither of them would be home for any length of time. Even if they bought a house in Cole's Hill after the selection phase—which a number of the candidates were thinking of doing if they were chosen for a future mission—they'd both always be focused on the mission. She didn't want to give going to space up and knew it would be unfair to ask him.

But a house, a life, maybe even kids one day—whoa. She'd never seen herself as a mom. Was she thinking that seriously? They'd slept together a few times and had just decided to give dating a try. This was why she'd dated only men who liked to keep things casual. She picked up the keys and hurried back upstairs.

She was still thinking of Velosi and his wife while she and Antonio ate.

"Are you okay?" he asked.

She nodded.

"I think we should head back to the facility as soon as we can," she said. Now that it was daylight, she felt exposed. She was still trying to figure out how to be a couple in private, and she wasn't too sure she was ready to be part of one in public.

"Okay. I think Carly will be missing me, as well. I know Ace will feed and walk her, but she likes to play," Antonio said.

"You're very sweet with that dog," Izzy said.

"I read an article that said a pet's bond with their owner was so deep because of the unconditional love the pet gives. There's no tension with a pet. It's just happy to see you whenever you walk into a room."

She wondered if he was trying to say that there was drama with her. And there was, she had to admit it. But she decided to leave some of that old baggage behind for now. She wasn't going to worry anymore about how her mom had never been able to make a relationship last. She'd been afraid for too long. "Cats can be kind of aloof," she said, not giving voice to her decision.

"Good point." As he finished, he said, "I'll be right back," and went into the other room to gather his things. She pushed the rest of her egg-white omelet around on her plate. She hadn't been hungry this morning. She was tired and emotional. A part of her wondered if she might be starting her period, but she knew it wasn't that time of the month. That would be a nice reason for her to be so…just so moody.

When they had packed up their few belongings, they headed downstairs. She was ready to get back to work.

She had been told by Hemi that the two teams would be brought back together after the next rotation through the simulator and the ranch duties. They'd compete one-on-one. They'd planned a steer-roping competition for all the candidates on the Memorial Day weekend.

Just as everyone else had, she'd been practicing with some help from one of the ranch hands. He was a champion roper and a great teacher. His skills were pretty good. Izzy saw a lot of similarities between roping and trying to hit a target in space. The variables were different, but the hand-eye coordination was similar, as was reading the terrain to ensure hitting the target the first time.

"Are you ready to go, *querida*?"

Antonio smiled and her breath caught, reminding her why she was here with him. It didn't matter if she felt awkward in public. She liked being with him and talking to him. Dating would make her feel odd because she had a hard time trusting men—and herself.

Damn. She'd always pretended that her upbringing hadn't really affected her, though she knew that it had. She didn't trust easily, and too many men had disappointed her more times than she wanted to acknowledge.

She knew that this was different. Antonio wasn't the same as the guys her mom dated, but at the same time she felt scared at how happy his being happy had made her. She wanted to be cautious, but it seemed that when it came to love, caution wasn't as easy as she had always assumed.

Still, she wasn't one to let fear stop her, and she had made a commitment to Antonio to see this through.

ANTONIO AND IZZY parted ways at the bunkhouse and he went up to the main ranch house to retrieve Carly.

He changed into a pair of faded Levi's and put on his boots before grabbing his cowboy hat and heading out the door.

The Texas sun was hot in mid-May and he was glad for the Stetson, which kept most of it off his face. The ranch house had a large front porch with rocking chairs that invited visitors to sit down. It reminded him of his mom's front porch, the same way the kitchen garden reminded him of home. Though the growing season and plants were different here there was something familiar about it.

And after his night with Izzy and spending too much time thinking instead of sleeping, he needed something that felt comforting…like home.

He rang the doorbell and heard Carly's bark and someone's footsteps. The door opened and a rush of cool air surrounded him. He smiled at the housekeeper, Rina, whom he'd met when he'd first come to the facility.

"Hello, Antonio. I guess you're here for this little cutie," she said.

"I am."

He stooped to pet the little dorgi, whose entire body was wagging. She licked his face and Antonio let the happiness of being greeted by the dog wash over him.

"Can I interest you in some iced tea?" Rina asked.

"Nah, I've got some studying to do before tomorrow morning. Thank you for watching this little one for me."

"It was my pleasure. Anytime you need a dog sitter, just give me a ring," she said.

Antonio patted the side of his leg and Carly came to heel next to him. He tipped his hat and said goodbye to

Rina, taking the path that led to the lake and not back to the bunkhouses. He wasn't quite ready to be back in his room alone with his thoughts. The ranch was empty this afternoon, probably due to the heat, and as he approached the lake Antonio heard the sounds of rock music cranked up and lots of splashing.

Carly looked up at him, tail wagging like she wanted to join in on the swimming. He used a hand motion to tell her no and kept walking toward the dock. He noticed the group was made up of ranch hands and they waved when they saw him.

"Hey, Playboy, you sure you're an astronaut?" one of them called out.

He realized he looked more like a hand than an astronaut this afternoon. "No, I'm with the Cronus program."

"Damn. You look like the real thing. You're still welcome to join us."

It was something he and his brothers had done many times on a hot summer day. "Don't mind if I do. Is the dog okay in the water?"

"Won't bother us," one of them said.

He motioned for Carly to go in, and she barked excitedly before running down the dock and throwing herself into the lake.

He stripped down to his boxers and jumped in, too. The men had a lot of questions about the program, and Antonio was happy to answer them.

"So Jason is the guy in charge of everything?"

It took him a moment to remember that Jason was Ace's real name. "He's the commander of the first mission and he serves a dual role as a head trainer," Antonio said as he floated on his back and looked up at the bright blue Texas sky. There wasn't a cloud to mar it.

"Have you spent any time with Jessie Odell?" one of them asked. "She's so badass. Every time we have one of those group get-togethers I try to get her alone, but her fiancé is always right there."

Antonio had to laugh. "Yeah, Hemi is a mite protective of her. I've really only had classes with her, and her training is invaluable. I've learned a lot."

"How is that going to help you in space?" another guy asked.

"We don't know what we will encounter or if one of the systems will fail. We will be a long way from Earth, so we need to know how to survive in extreme temperatures or when things break. She is teaching us how to react to things we aren't expecting," Antonio said.

"Playboy!"

Antonio stopped floating on his back and turned to face the shore. When he saw Ace and Dr. Tomlin standing onshore, he immediately swam toward them.

"What's up?" he asked as he approached them.

"Doc Tomlin had an appointment open up for bone-density testing and you haven't had a scan in the last ten days, so we hunted you down," Ace said.

"Sorry, Ace, did I miss something? I thought I had nothing on my schedule." He whistled for Carly, and then got out of the water and gathered his things.

"Not a big deal. She came up to the house to tell me and Rina had mentioned you had just been there. Seemed like it might be convenient to have you take the slot."

"I'd love to," Antonio said. "Let's go."

Dr. Tomlin smiled at him. She was in her mid-thirties with curly brown hair and a very easy smile. She teased, "I think we have enough time for you to put your clothes back on."

In the summer-Texas heat he was almost dry. He pulled on his jeans easily but left the buttons on his shirt undone as he sat down to put on his boots. Carly sat patiently next to him.

"Which test is this?" he asked as they headed back to the facility. Ace had returned to the ranch house already. They all had routine tests that were run on them every week.

"It's a baseline so we can establish your levels. I will be measuring your reactions against another candidate. Really, that's why we needed you now. The test works best when I have two subjects to examine."

"Who is the other candidate?"

"Izzy Wolsten," Dr. Tomlin said. "Stephen Miller had to bow out for now."

Of course it was. He wanted some time away to think and put everything in perspective, so of course the universe was forcing them together.

Dr. Tomlin's office always reminded Izzy of some sort of futuristic laboratory. Not that Doc Tomlin was ever anything other than nice. But before she was even permitted to get on the machines, she had to put on a special suit and have pads that were similar to the ones used in EKGs placed on her skin. It took a good thirty minutes to get ready to just go into the lab.

Her normal testing partner was sick this morning, and she'd been sitting in the antechamber of the lab for a while when the door opened and Antonio walked in.

"Hello."

"Hiya. So how'd you get dragged into this?" she asked. "I thought this was a red-team thing."

"I was available so Ace moved me into the vacant spot," he said. "You make these weird frog suits look good."

She shook her head. "Flattery? I've seen myself in the mirror. No one looks good in these things."

Right now they were covered from neck to ankle in a suit similar in looks to a wet suit. Once they got inside they'd be strapped into the AlterG machine to run first without oxygen and then with it. The results were compared to their own baseline results and to others in the group.

Because atmospheric variables could influence the results, Dr. Tomlin tested them in pairs to see if the results were both in the same range.

"Are you trying to say this isn't my best look?" he asked.

"Well, you looked a lot better last night," she said.

"As did you."

Doc Tomlin joined them before she could take the conversation down another dangerous path. But her mind was filled of images of Antonio as he'd looked sitting on the chair last night with his shirt off...

"Izzy, I'll take you in first and get you set up in the machine. Antonio, my assistant Patrick will be here in a minute to get you," Doc Tomlin said.

She led Izzy into the room and over to the AlterG machine, a specially designed treadmill that had a section in the middle that simulated zero gravity. It helped them to work out in the way they would on the machines that were installed on their vehicle for the Cronus missions. Because of the lack of gravity, the bones in the body would become weakened after long months in space, which would have a major impact when they returned to earth. So testing was a paramount part of this facility. They were also researching solutions that might work long-term. As mission commander, Ace had logged over a year on the ISS before coming here and was himself part of the experiment.

The machine on the space station was a bit easier to get into, and normally they didn't wear the extra sensors that Dr. Tomlin had them use here.

"When did you take the calcium shake?" Doc Tomlin asked, her clipboard in hand.

"Thirty minutes before I arrived for the test," Izzy answered.

She continued to answer the doctor's questions as she was helped onto the machine and the sensors were connected so that up-to-the-second readings could be taken. She tried to focus on the questions and on her job. But she knew the moment that Antonio was taken to his machine and was a little bit distracted by the warm rumble of his voice.

She had that warm feeling in her stomach that she got whenever she thought about him or when he was close by. She let herself enjoy the feeling but not be distracted by it, and somehow found it easy to focus on the doctor and her questions. She knew she and Antonio were both here to do their jobs, and there was something that felt right about that deep in her soul.

She looked over at Antonio only once and noticed that he was watching her. He winked at her and she shook her head.

"Okay. It's not really a competition," Dr. Tomlin said, "but we are keeping total track of your miles and, of course, your speed. This will help me with your body's reactions. We do have a leaderboard, and right now Hennessey is at the top of it. Not really surprising since he runs marathons and is used to endurance running.

"I am going to count down from five. The lights on your machine will flash three times and then stay lit, at which point the treadmill will begin to move and you will start running," Doc Tomlin said. "Any questions?"

"What is the target?" Antonio asked.

"Just do your best," she said, instead of giving a real number.

"Doc, you said Hennessey was top," Izzy added. "How did he do?"

"You will be able to see him simulated on the screen in front of you. Just move along and keep up with him as best you can," Doc Tomlin said before walking out of the room into her observation office with her staff.

"Keep up?" Izzy said. "I'm going to blow him away."

"Only if you are keeping up with me," Antonio said.

"Wanna bet?"

"Sure. Loser has to do one thing that winner chooses?" he suggested.

"Agreed. I hope you don't mind taking over my early-morning ranching chores, because I could use a day to sleep in."

"Me, too," he said. "But I have something more intimate in mind."

"Like what?" she asked, paying closer attention to Antonio than she was the machine.

"Washing Carly," he said, as the lights started flashing and the screen in front of them flickered to life. A blue silhouette representing Hennessey appeared, with his time in blue.

"Deal."

She turned away from Antonio and to something that she could always rely on. A challenge. Pitting herself against someone and winning. That was one thing she'd always been good at and she needed this, she thought. After the self-doubt she'd been wrestling with, she needed a win.

She hoped that Antonio was as strong as she thought he was, because she wasn't backing down.

11

MERE SECONDS SEPARATED Izzy and Antonio on the AlterG machine leaderboard, and that wasn't the only challenge where they were neck and neck. Two weeks ago, the teams had switched, and Antonio had enjoyed his time riding fence with the ranch hands. There was something soothing about being on the back of a horse, and it put him in touch with his roots in a way that he hadn't been in years.

He also hated it slightly. Being out in the pasture gave him too much time to think about Izzy. They were still "dating," though he used the term loosely. They had crashed in each other's rooms a few times over the last two weeks, but Ace and Hemi were driving all of the candidates hard and some of those evenings had been quickie sex followed by deep sleep.

He admitted to himself that having her in his arms at night made him sleep better. Probably because she was the number-one cause of his insomnia when she wasn't there. When he held her, he felt almost like he really had her. He knew he didn't, though. Had glimpsed the competitive glean in her eyes too many times to ever think that they were going to drift into some kind of solid relationship.

This was his last day of dedicated ranch chores. Tomorrow was the start of Memorial Day weekend, and there was a combination of events on the Bar T and in town that everyone was taking part in. There was a mock rodeo tomorrow and all of the Cronus candidates would be taking part in a dummy steer-roping competition, followed by some exhibition bull riding and barrel racing. Then a barbecue by the lake and dancing. He'd be competing against Izzy at the steer roping, and then cleaning up and coming to the party as a couple.

He'd sent away for a gift for her because he wanted her to know that he saw her as more than someone who egged him on. Someone who made him better because he was always striving to keep up with her. He wanted to get her something personal that would remind her of him and ultimately of them when they were apart.

When he got back from checking this section of fence he was going to see if the package had been delivered. He also needed to check his weekly email. With his brothers' help, he was trying to arrange a trip to the state for his parents so they could see where he trained. They would have to stay in Cole's Hill, but Antonio's family was very close and it had been over a year since he'd been able to get home.

"Dude, you are taking your time staring at that fence. Does it need to be repaired?" Marty asked.

Marty was a tall and lanky cowboy and had been the

one to confess to having a crush on Jessie Odell that day Antonio had gone swimming with the hands. He was a laconic speaker with a dry wit and ribald sense of humor. Antonio liked working with him.

"Sorry, Marty. The fence is fine over here," Antonio said.

"You look like a man with a lot on his mind," Marty said as they started riding back toward the Bar T's main barn.

"You could say that."

"Are you worried about going so far away from Earth?" Marty asked. "I've been following the press briefings on the Cronus mission. I'd be scared shitless if I was up there in space for a day, much less eighteen months."

Antonio thought about it. Sure, there were moments when he experienced some trepidation. Like when the launch vehicle tests failed or when he heard rumors that the stationary jets on the actual space station still weren't working, but overall the call to be out there in space overshadowed that.

"Not really," Antonio said. "My brothers all think I'm crazy, though."

"They ain't the only ones," Marty said with a laugh.

They got back to the barn and groomed their horses before Antonio left to go check and see if his mail had arrived. As he approached the ranch house, he heard laughter. Lots of women, he thought. And then he heard Izzy. He came around the corner of the house where the back porch led to a deck and the pool. His eyes were drawn to Izzy in her bikini lying on a chaise next to Meredith, Molly and Rina.

They were talking about something, but it wasn't the words that he listened to. It was the joy. He realized he'd only seen glimpses of this side of Izzy, and it made him aware of the fact that she was on guard with him. The only time he really had a chance to know her and see her like this was when they were making love.

Outside of the bedroom she always kept her distance. He wasn't sure if it was a conscious thing or not, but he decided he had to get to the bottom of it.

He cleared his throat and the women all turned to look at him.

"Hello, Antonio," Rina called out. "This is a girls-only party, but we might make an exception for you if you have your cute dog with you."

"I'm alone, I'm afraid. I don't mean to intrude, but I was expecting a package to be delivered today," Antonio said.

"Yep, I saw something come in for you," Rina called back. "Follow me, and I'll get it for you."

He approached the deck and noticed that Izzy hadn't said a word to him. A part of him was tired of the to-and-fro that was going on between them. He knew they'd been training hard and maybe she just needed this time with her friends to unwind and relax, but he needed her to acknowledge him.

Because despite what she'd said, he'd been the one to go to her on the nights they'd spent together. And he was beginning to believe that no matter what she'd said, all she wanted from him was a booty call.

Izzy watched Antonio walk away, knowing she should have said something. He looked good. Hot and dusty from spending a day working the ranch. His olive skin had darkened in the sun and his shirt fit his shoulders and muscled arms like a second skin. His jeans were faded and looked soft as they clung to his body in all the right places.

So, instead of talking, she'd hid behind her sunglasses and just watched him. Listened to the deep rumble of his voice and his accent, and had a flashback to him reading to her in the bathtub.

She was struggling. Only on the nights when he knocked on her door was she able to let go for a few minutes and allow him in. Not only into her room but also into her life.

The competition was stiff between them, but it wasn't just that keeping her from him. It was her own fears and her desire to not stumble this close to the finish line.

She'd realized it this morning when she'd been in the simulator of the actual space vehicle they would be using on the mission working with assembling part of the space station in the underwater tank. She had read over Antonio's notes, which he'd been so generous to share with her and the rest of her team, and she realized that as much as she'd always worked in a group, she didn't like to have to rely on anyone else. She had always been at the front of the pack because she didn't trust those around her. She had to lead.

Which was uncomfortable when she realized it was true in her personal life, as well. Though she had wanted to go to Antonio's room every night, she refused to be the one to break first or to show that she needed him.

She was playing a game and she was smart enough to know that if she played with a real relationship she was going to get burned. She wasn't ready to admit that she and Antonio could be more than friends or lovers. No matter what she'd said in those predawn hours at the Grand Hotel, the truth was that she wasn't ready.

She wanted to be. When she was with Antonio he made her trust that she had nothing to fear, but her demons had been with her longer than anything else. They were familiar. She wanted to believe she was the strong woman she saw herself as, that she'd never crumble because of a man and wasn't cut from the same cloth as her mom.

But here she was watching Antonio walk away and feeling a pang deep in her stomach. A longing for him. Every time it sprang up, she tried to convince herself it was only sexual, but that was a lie. They hadn't had a chance to just hang out and talk lately, and she missed that as much as she missed the sex when she wasn't with him.

This was more than sex.

Pretending otherwise was an insult to Antonio and to herself. "Excuse me, ladies."

She jumped up and followed Rina and Antonio into the house. The air-conditioning felt cold after the outside heat, and the tile floor was cool on her feet. She followed the sound of Rina's voice to find them standing in the main hallway. Suddenly, she had no idea what she was going to say.

"Antonio, are you going back to the bunkhouse?"

"I am," he said.

"Wait for me, I'd like to go with you," Izzy said.

Rina raised her eyebrow but only said, "I'll keep him company while you grab your shoes and bag."

Izzy nodded before turning and going back outside to gather her things. She pulled on her gauzy beach cover-up and picked up her bag. "Sorry to bail, ladies, but I haven't had a chance to talk to Antonio for a few days."

"It's okay," Meredith said. "We'll miss you."

Izzy stood there, not entirely sure what to say, but having already committed to Antonio she knew she couldn't waffle on it now. But going public hadn't been part of her plan. Meredith was in the Cronus program. Was it wise to imply that she and Antonio were involved? There was a lot risk involved with dating someone else on the team.

"Thanks," Izzy said. She felt stupid. Was she the only woman in the world who was this messed up and confused about a man? Why was this so hard? Now that she knew Antonio, she knew he was a good guy. He had manners, he was smart, he was funny, he didn't get mad when she won, and better still, didn't let her win. He had a rocking, sexy bod. He was everything a woman could ask for.

Yet, she'd been holding herself back.

She wished she could just let go, but she couldn't. The more she tried, the more she dug in her heels.

Idiot.

She'd been keeping herself aloof from him, but she needed to just enjoy this. She regretted not at least living with one of her boyfriends in the past; maybe then this wouldn't feel so foreign and she'd know how to just be with Antonio.

But there had never been a man who made her feel what Antonio did. And as much as she was unsure and apprehensive about him, she also couldn't simply walk away or let him go.

She wasn't thinking about the space program or anything other than Antonio.

Was this what it was like for her mom? Was this why she'd sworn off men?

Izzy wanted to ask her, but then that would mean opening up a bunch of issues from her upbringing that she had never wanted to deal with.

She walked back through the house to where Rina and Antonio waited.

"Ready to go?"

"Yes, ma'am," he said.

ANTONIO TUCKED HIS package under his arm as they walked back toward the training facility and the bunkhouse quad. Izzy didn't say anything as she kept pace beside him. She smelled like summer to him—a combination of coconut and pineapple. He assumed it was her sunscreen.

He wanted to ask her about her past. To figure out why she was so gun-shy when it came to him. But, of course, that would be opening up a can of worms that he might not like. Instead, he searched for something else—something safe—to talk about.

"We're both at the top of the leaderboard in skills,"

he said. "I hope that means we are both chosen for the first mission."

"Me, too," she said, then reached out and took his hand.

Hers was clammy and she sort of clung to his hand. He slowed his pace and looked down at their joined hands, then over at her.

"Are you okay?"

She shook her head. "I'm not. Not even close. I told you I would be okay with dating, and then I slunk back to my room, working every hour I could in order to make sure I was exhausted every night so I wouldn't be tempted to go to you. But the only time I sleep is when you come to my room. I'm running from you and I'm starting to think I should be running *to* you."

Antonio took a deep breath and pulled her to a stop near one of the large shade trees that dotted the path. There was a small wrought-iron bench underneath it, and he drew her over to it. This was the kind of conversation that needed to be had in private and in a neutral area. Not the bunkhouse.

"Why? What is it about me that scares you so much?" he asked. "I'm trying to give you room and let you set the pace, but even that doesn't help."

She pursed her lips and looked down at her lap. "I've never really had time for relationships, and I've put them on the back burner for a reason."

He lifted their joined hands and brushed a kiss along the back of her knuckles. "Whatever it is, I'm not going to run away."

"You should. I'm carrying around so much baggage."

"We all are," he said. "That's how we know this is serious. We're adults, and we've got the scars and the triumphs to prove it."

She tipped her head to the side and studied him with her large gray eyes. He didn't want to admit to falling for the wrong woman in the past or the fact that there were times he wasn't sure he could live up to the example his parents had set of what a couple should be. But his own relationships with women had always left him feeling wounded and raw. Never giving him that love and commitment he saw in his parents.

They both made each other stronger, and while he and Izzy pushed each other to improve at their jobs, Antonio had no idea if he made her a better person.

"That's very wise," she said. "Sometimes I feel I'm the only one who is a big mess inside."

"If only," he said. "The older I get the more I realize that almost everyone is a mess. All we can do is try our best. Tell me what you fear."

"I sort of started to the other night and then chickened out," she said.

Whatever she was hiding from was deeply embedded in her. He knew because he'd spent a lot of hours running from his own demons and knew what that looked like.

He took a deep breath. He wanted to make it easier for her. Wasn't that what a man was supposed to do for the woman he loved?

But he'd been the one to reach out every time. She always welcomed him, but he needed her to take the first step once in a while.

She nibbled on her bottom lip and then inhaled audibly. "I had five stepdads when I was growing up. My mom is a very good mother—so please don't think I'm judging her—but she didn't know how to live without a man in her life. Actually, I think she's still not sure how to deal with men and so I've never really trusted a relationship."

That was something he wasn't expecting. Five stepdads…that was a lot. He remembered his own childhood with his steady parents and brothers, and he felt the guilt over his own demons grow. She could have taken a different path; instead, she was stronger than he was.

"Were they good to you?" he asked.

"Some of them. And there were guys she dated in between. Some of them just ignored me, some had kids of their own. It was complicated. My mom always changed with each new relationship, losing herself in the man of the moment. I vowed I'd never do that."

He could see that. "I can't imagine you ever letting a man have that much control over you."

"I'm glad you think that. But I am afraid to let myself really care about you, Antonio. I'm afraid if I let go for a second, then I will be just like my mom." She ran her hand through her hair and shook her head. "I love my mom and I'm not trying to diss her, but what if that's just the way we are? You're the first man that I've even thought of in a serious way and I am afraid of that. Afraid of you."

Her truth humbled him, and he wished there was something he could say to reassure her. But he wasn't sure of what the future held. He'd never ask her to be anything other than herself, but until she was really committed to him, she'd never know if she had that capability.

12

SHE FELT LIGHTER now that she'd told him what was going on. It made her feel even better that Antonio didn't push her fears aside or tell her that they'd be fine. She saw in him the truth of what he'd said earlier. That they were made up of their scars and experiences, and because of that they both knew there were no easy answers.

She squeezed his hand in hers.

"I feel better. Thank you for listening," she said. "Another problem of mine is I hate to admit I'm not perfect."

"I think most of us have that problem," he said sardonically.

"Really? Even you?" she said with a wink.

He threw his head back and laughed. "Says the woman who insists on getting into the gym after me every damned day and beating my scores."

"Just trying to keep you on your toes," she said. Which was only partially her motivation for doing it. In reality, she hadn't wanted to run into him in the gym and chance her own willpower weakening.

"What about you? Anything that's keeping you back?" she asked. "Though you do seem pretty willing to keep coming after me."

His smile wasn't genuine. She wasn't sure how she could tell, exactly, except that it didn't reach his eyes and there was something stiff about the way he sat next to her. The air of relaxation and comfort he'd been projecting dissipated.

"Let's save that for another time," he said.

She didn't want to push, but having just bared her soul she wished he felt safe enough to do the same. Though she wanted to keep things even between them, that wasn't the way life worked and she knew it. However, it didn't stop her from being slightly upset that he wasn't going to tell her his secrets.

"Is this payback?" she asked. She didn't know Antonio well enough to guess at his reasons here, but she wanted him to know he could talk to her about his own fears.

"For?"

"For me and the way I've been acting the last two weeks," she said. "Is this your way of evening the scales?"

"No. What kind of man do you think I am?" he asked, dropping her hand and standing up. He turned his back to her and put his hands on his hips. His shoulders drooped and he put his head down.

"I don't know," she said. "To be fair, you don't know the kind of woman I am. I might have been using you for sex."

He glanced over his shoulder at her, his expression

obscured by the shadow cast by the brim of his Stetson. "I had considered that."

"That's fair, though it does hurt a little. I was scared."

"I know," he said. "My issues…aren't like yours. But they are just as dangerous."

She realized that he wasn't ready to trust her with whatever he had in his past. Yet. She hoped it would be *yet* and not never.

"Fair enough," she said. "Let's go back to the bunkhouse. I'm free for the rest of the evening. What's your schedule like?"

"Free," he said. "Why?"

"Put on something pretty and meet me in the quad at six," she said.

"Something pretty?" he asked, turning to face her. "Do you know how condescending that sounds?"

"Yup," she said, getting up, walking over and patting him on the ass. "Guys have been saying stuff like that to women for years."

He caught her around the waist, pulling her off her feet and against his body. "Women like it, right?"

She mock punched him because she knew he was joking. "No, they don't."

"Well, what about surprises? Do women like surprises?" he asked. "Because I have one for you."

She wrapped her arms around his neck and kissed him. "The fact that you want me isn't a surprise."

"How can you be sure?" he asked.

She rocked her pelvis against his and tipped her head to the side. "You're giving yourself away, buddy."

"Buddy? Do I look like a *buddy* to you?" he asked

as he set her on her feet. He picked up his parcel off the bench and took her hand as they started walking back to the bunkhouses.

"Not really. But I'm not sure what to call you, *babe*?"

"Again with these words that women seem to find offensive," he said.

"I don't mind if you call me *babe*," she said. "But I really enjoy it when you call me *querida*. Your voice deepens when you speak Spanish. It's very sexy."

He started speaking to her in Spanish immediately. She understood about a third of it, but it made her feel good. She hadn't lost herself by being herself with him, and she'd found a way to coax him back from the edge of whatever was bothering him. She didn't have a definite idea for the evening except that she'd seen a bar in Cole's Hill when they'd driven through the other day, and Ace had told her when he was growing up they'd had a bunch of game machines and a mechanical bull inside. She thought it might be fun to take this cowboy on a date.

"Are you turned-on?" he asked.

"By you? Always," she said. "That's never been the issue, has it?"

"No, it hasn't. So…what are we doing tonight?"

"Don't you worry your pretty little head about anything, babe, I've got it all covered," she said, giving him a hard kiss on the lips and walking into the bunkhouse ahead of him.

She could do this, she thought. She'd just keep it smooth and easy, and soon enough she'd figure out how to do this relationship thing. Though there was a niggling doubt when she remembered the darkness in Antonio earlier. She'd worry about that later. She had to sort herself out first before she figured him out.

COLE'S HILL HAD been listed as one of the fastest growing small towns in the US a few years ago and Antonio could see why. It was a quaint mixture of historic, restored buildings on the main street and large minimansion subdivisions on the outskirts.

There was the Grand Hotel where they'd had the party earlier in the month, and then a larger facility near the town square. Izzy drove her Mustang through the streets a little bit fast but with complete control, which was to be expected.

Just past the town square and the Five Families area, she signaled left and turned down a road that was lined with more historic old buildings including one with a flashing neon sign that read The Bull Pit. She pulled into a parking lot full of SUVs and pickup trucks and parked the Mustang in the corner away from the other vehicles.

"This isn't what I was expecting," he said.

"Good. I don't want to be predictable."

He didn't say anything as he followed her into the roadhouse. Antonio could tell from the vehicles in the parking lot that this wasn't a dive bar, and when they got inside the atmosphere was one of rowdy fun. He followed her through the large bar area, partially watching where they were heading, but mostly observing the sway of her hips in the skintight jeans she wore. She had on a pink plaid Western shirt and a straw cowgirl hat. She wore Tony Lama boots, and she had a hand-tooled leather belt that had Bombshell burned into the back of it.

She stopped abruptly and he put his hands on her waist as he realized they'd reached their destination.

"Fancy a ride on this?" she asked.

He looked at the mechanical bull and then back down at Izzy. "Hell, yeah. In fact, I'll wager I can stay on longer than you."

"I hoped you'd say that. The loser pays for dinner," she said.

"Deal."

They put their names on the list to ride the bull and had to read and sign a waiver. They glanced at each other as they signed it, knowing that Ace wouldn't approve if he knew what they were doing.

"Technically, no one said we couldn't do it," she said. "And tonight I want to be us. Not two candidates on a strict schedule. But if you think we shouldn't do it, just say."

He shook his head. Like Izzy, he wanted them to be just a guy and a girl. They needed this time to forget about the pressure of the program and the reality that if either of them was chosen, they would soon be locked into a program for the next ten years of their lives. Plus, the mechanical-bull operation didn't seem that dangerous. There were pads on the floor and the operator could choose different setting levels.

He was pretty sure they would both walk away from their ride.

There was something a little smug about Izzy's smile as she handed the clipboard back to the attendant.

"Have you done this before?" he asked.

"Possibly," she said.

She was being minx-like. It was as if by telling him that she wasn't going to be perfect at the whole relationship thing, she'd freed herself. He wished it could be as easy for him. He was enjoying this side of Izzy. He just hoped she was being true to herself…but then, she had said she didn't know who she would be. She might be trying out a bunch of different things.

It struck him how lucky he was to be the first man Izzy felt this way about. The first man to experience her as she was letting go for the first time. She made him feel…well, special in a way that he never had before.

"Possibly? In the spirit of that answer, I may or may not have been the champion at my local bar back in Buenos Aires."

"What? Are you kidding?"

"Nope. It was the one thing I really liked. Dad took us to a rodeo when it was on tour and my brothers and I were hooked. We weren't allowed in the bar at night, but Dad was friends with the owner, so he'd bring us in during the afternoon if we'd done all of our chores and homework," Antonio said.

"Dang, I think I should have asked for a story before I booked this. But I will let you go first so I know what time I have to beat," she said.

"A story?" he asked, more intrigued by that than competing with her. They'd spent a lot of time in competition with each other, but stories were different.

"Yes. I was saving it for dinner, but I thought we could each exchange stories that have nothing to do with the space program. We know each other's history there…well, most of it. I don't know why you left NASA," she said.

And hopefully she never would. That was one of the darkest and most shameful times in his life and he really wasn't prepared to talk about it.

"You're already into me for one story, so that will have to wait for now. Are you sure you don't want to go first?"

"Yes. I want to see how good you are, maybe pick up a few tips from watching you," she said.

He'd bet she was already pretty good and he knew that, as with anything with Izzy, he needed to be sharp and focused, not dwelling in the past and in regrets. He was proud of the man he was today. The baggage and the scars were just part of the package. He wasn't going to let himself get sucked back into regrets.

The attendant gestured him to the bull and he felt Izzy's hand on the small of his back. He looked over his shoulder at her and she went up on her tiptoes and hugged him. He wrapped his arm around her quickly before letting go.

"Be safe."

SHE COULDN'T BEAT him on the mechanical bull, but that didn't matter at all since she was enjoying the evening a lot. They found a table toward the back of the bar. He ordered barbecue beef brisket with fried okra and she opted for mac and cheese, something she loved but only let herself eat on special occasions since she had an hourglass figure, which meant everything showed on her hips.

Antonio had gotten stewed apples and greens as his sides, and they had decided to have one glass of sweet iced tea before switching back to water. She was enjoying seeing Antonio this way, and, even more, she was enjoying herself.

In the past, instead of enjoying dinner she would have insisted they play pool or darts or any of the video games at the front of the bar until she'd beaten him so she could show him they were equals. But that no longer seemed paramount. She was enjoying this new part of herself and her time with him.

He was funny and at times quiet, and since she was being so open, she started to notice that there were some subjects that made Antonio go quiet. Her mind, which was always analyzing, had been narrowing down the topics, and she figured that something must have happened with Antonio when she'd been on her mission with the ISS. He had been scheduled on a later mission than hers, and when she'd returned for one of the long-term training sessions, he had been in Hawaii. She hadn't been around when he'd left NASA.

He avoided talking about that time, though he would talk about their early training-class days and the later stuff with Space Now, which he was doing now.

"Malcolm Pennington is one of those men who doesn't really care about the cost, only the end result, so you'd think he'd be all buttoned up and business all the time, but he's not. He's maybe five years older than we are. And crazy as all get-out," Antonio said.

"Give me an example of his crazy," she said.

"He wanted to see if we could launch from the atmosphere—the idea came from one of the finalists in his 'get us to space, win a million dollars' competition. So the guy who had this theory suggested we use rockets to launch the space station up into orbit, and then use solar balloons to get the astronauts up there. Then we'd have to meet up with the orbiting station and board it."

Izzy didn't like the sound of that. "Wouldn't that be dangerous? There are a lot of variables that would have to be accounted for."

"Exactly, so Mal said we can't have one of you guys trying it, you're too valuable. Instead, he arranged to try to 'board' one of his own satellites. He wouldn't actually board it, just rendezvous with it by solar balloon and see if it was possible to connect."

"Did it work?" she asked.

"No. But he tried it. And he's crazy, so once he did, on his way back down, he free-fell from the lower atmosphere to break a world record. When I went to work for him I knew it would be different," Antonio said.

"Why didn't you come back to NASA?" she asked.

"I didn't feel that door was open to me," he said. "I'm glad they considered me for Cronus."

He fiddled with his cell phone, not looking at her.

"Why? Talk to me, babe. Tell me what's really going on," she said. "Because you are really good at what you do. Why would they even think of not bringing you on?"

"It was more me than them. I had… I guess it's more accurate to say I *have* a drinking problem. You missed it because you were on the ISS and then wherever you went after, but I crashed and burned pretty hard after training. And they—NASA—gave me a leave of absence to get my shit together. I did, but I was too embarrassed to come back, and I wasn't sure they'd have me if I tried. I didn't want a replay of what had happened before. I wasn't sure… I wasn't sure I'd be able to handle the pressure."

"But now you are?" she asked. This news was unexpected and didn't fit at all with the Antonio she knew. But a lot of demons were private. Hadn't they discussed that?

"I am," Antonio said. "Actually, I'm in a lot better place now. I was in a destructive relationship the last time, which had driven a wedge between myself and my family. We brought out the worst in each other… Anyway, enough of that. I didn't mean to tell you," he said. "Especially not here."

"I think you needed to," she said. "I get you a little better now. Want to take off? I have a few more things planned for this evening."

He gave her a long, hard look, then nodded and stood up. She took his hand and thought about the future, and how sure she had to be of her actions. She would never have wanted to hurt Antonio before this, but now that she understood how vulnerable he was, she had better be careful around him. But now she saw she might have hurt him by doing that.

Some of the doubt she'd had about their relationship

crept back in, and though she tried to regain her happy attitude, she knew it was gone. Like everything, her attitude had been changed by facts and experience. She drove them out of Cole's Hill and when they reached the Bar T, she drove down a rutted dirt road that led to a hill that gave them a nice view of the night sky without any light pollution from town or the ranch and the Mick Tanner facility.

She parked the car and then turned to Antonio. "Want to lay on a blanket with me and count stars?"

13

THE SKY WAS full of stars tonight and as they settled on the blanket, Antonio still wasn't sure how he'd managed to share with Izzy the secret he had been keeping for a long time. She was acting again. Trying her best to be normal and pretend that things were the same, but having seen that tiny glimpse into the genuine woman, he could tell the difference now.

And it hurt to think he'd caused the change.

His drinking had been his one source of weakness for a long time. But he was better. Much better. "I've been sober for more than five years now, Bombshell. You don't have to worry about me screwing up on a mission."

She turned her head slightly to look at him. He wished he could see her expression more clearly, but his eyes hadn't adjust to the dark yet.

"I'm not worried about that. You wouldn't be here in Cole's Hill if anyone thought there was even the slightest chance that you were going to lose it."

"Then what are you worried about?" he asked, placing his hands behind him on the blanket and leaning back on his elbows. He looked up at the sky, which was easier to decipher than this woman was.

"That I'll hurt you. That I'll do something destructive because I can't handle us, and it will affect not only our personal lives but our professional ones, as well. I don't want that to happen. Not at all."

"Don't worry about it," he said.

"So does that mean you think I won't hurt you?" she asked, leaning back on her elbows next to him.

"I know you don't want to, and I think whatever happens between us is going to do so at its own pace, and there is little we can do to control it."

She turned on her side to face him. "I don't believe that. We are two of the most deliberate people on the planet. I've never known you to do something without analyzing all the possible outcomes."

"True. But you aren't a mission and the parameters for dating as I know it have shifted. You're different, Izzy."

"Good," she said. "I'd hate to be like everyone else."

"Don't worry, you aren't," he said. "Why did you bring me out here?"

"To see who knows more constellations," she said. "I thought it would be fun to name them."

It would be, but since they were on a date and not just colleagues looking at the stars, he moved around until he was behind her and pulled her close. Her back rested against his chest and he wrapped his arms around her waist.

"Okay, so we can take turns naming them until one of us fails," she said. "I do have an app on my phone we can use in case we need an outside opinion."

"You want to go first?" he asked.

"Sure."

They took turns naming constellations, and each one seemed to bring a story with it. Izzy spotted Canis Major first. "This is actually the constellation that got me interested in astronomy and eventually led to the space program."

"Is it? Why?" he asked.

"My first stepdad, Randy, showed it to me when Mom was adamant that I wasn't getting a pet. He said, you don't need a dog on earth when you have this one in the heavens. He was a really nice guy. We sat in the backyard and he pointed it out to me and told me that the best thing about the night sky is that it would always be with me."

Antonio hugged her close to him. "Sounds like he was a pretty decent guy."

"He was. Unfortunately, he was nice to a few other ladies, too. Turned out Mom and I were one of three families he had," Izzy said.

"I'm sorry."

"Don't be. It was a long time ago and I found something that stuck with me for life because of him. Mom always says that everyone is sent into our lives to teach us something," Izzy said. "We learned a lot of lessons over the years."

"I like that idea," Antonio said. He thought of the

people in his life and how each one had made a difference in who he was and how he reacted to things.

"There's the Big Dipper," Antonio said.

"That's almost cheating it's so easy," she said.

"I'm sure you know that it's called by different names all over the world. Some of my favorites are the UK version, where it's called the Plough. And the Mayans called it the Parrot, while the ancient Egyptians saw it as part of a bull," he said.

"Isn't it fascinating how we all look up at the same sky and see so many different things?"

"I guess the sky is giving us what we need, what we want to see," he said.

"I think so. Part of the reason I became fascinated with the stars and other celestial bodies was reading about how they are a constant throughout human history."

Antonio agreed. They lay there for a while talking about their childhoods and remembering stories they'd heard or made up about constellations. And Antonio realized that he was falling for Izzy. The hope he'd had that maybe dating her would make it easier to walk away from her, well, maybe he'd never really believed that.

"There it is," he said, lifting his arm and pointing to Mars. "The planet that is going to be the focus of our lives from now on."

"I know. So hard to believe that in a few short years we are going to be halfway there. I love being a part of the space program because of that. Because we get to go after the things that once seemed impossible."

"I CHECKED EARLIER," Izzy said, "And the Comet C/2013 X1 PanSTARRS comet might be visible tonight. I've always wanted to see it while sitting under the stars with someone special. My mom isn't really interested in the night sky. So…"

"I'm glad you chose me," he said.

He leaned forward and rested his head on her shoulder, and she felt the heat of his breath against her cheek as he spoke. "I haven't seen that comet. I've spent most of my time in the lab or a simulator preparing for the mission in the last few years. I'd forgotten what it's like to be out here under the stars."

"I know what you mean," she said. "So much of what we do is focused on getting us ready to go that it's easy to lose touch of where we are going."

He shifted so they were lying on the blanket side by side, and she turned to face the direction that the comet was supposed to be easily viewed. Antonio moved behind her, wrapping one arm around her waist and putting the other under her head. She rested against him, liking the way his big frame supported her smaller one. And the way he held her made her feel safe and cared for.

She turned her head, dropping a kiss on his wrist, and then turned back to the sky. Antonio's hands drifted over her body, running along her side starting at her shoulder and down to her hip.

"I get the feeling that you aren't watching for the comet," she said.

"Do you mind? I can only hold you for so long before I want you," he admitted.

"Why would I mind that?" she asked, rolling to face him. She put her hands on his cheeks and dropped a kiss on the tip of his nose. "I like it."

She draped her thigh over his hips and he put his hand at the small of her back and pulled her closer to him. There was none of the urgency that had always dominated their lovemaking before. She wasn't sure if it was because they wanted to make things last or because they were starting to know each other's bodies better.

When their mouths met, she dipped her head to the right because she knew he liked to tip his head to the left. The kiss was long and slow and deep, building the tension inside. His hands skimmed down her back and then up again, the caress languid, making her melt into him.

He rolled her to her back and she opened her legs for him to nestle between. He rested the weight of his upper body on his elbows and broke their kiss to drop nibbling kisses along her jawline all the way to her ear, taking the lobe into his mouth and sucking on it.

He whispered hot words of sexual need and demand into her ear, which made her shiver with desire.

SLOWLY HE MADE his way back to her mouth, lightly rubbing his lips back and forth over hers. She felt the humid warmth of his exhalation in her mouth. He tasted so…delicious. Like the white-hot trail the PanSTARRS comet would leave behind, she felt that everywhere his hands moved left a wake of fiery need.

His taste was addictive. Nothing new there—he'd been addictive since the first time she'd touched him.

This felt safe, she thought. Lying in his arms, she knew what to do and how to behave. She didn't have to second-guess herself or try to pretend she was something she wasn't. This was where she felt they were the most honest with each other.

His hands moved across her shoulders, his fingers tracing a delicate pattern over the globes of her breasts. He moved them back and forth over the tops until the very tip of his finger dipped beneath the material of her top and reached lower, brushing the edge of her nipple.

Exquisite shivers racked her body as his finger continued its exploration. He found the buttons on her shirt and slowly undid them, pushing the fabric aside and then staring down at her. She wore a balconette bra, which lifted her breasts up and together and gave her cleavage a nice boost. He traced one finger over the exposed tops of her breasts.

He reached underneath her and undid the catch of her bra with one hand and then lifted her with that hand under her back.

"Take your blouse off," he said. His voice was almost guttural, it was so low and raw.

She shifted her shoulders until her arms were free of her blouse and bra. He lowered her to the blanket. It was soft against her shoulders, and his hands, as they moved up and down her torso, were hot and provocative. He cupped her breasts in each of his hands and ran his thumb around her areola. He felt her nipple bud and she shifted her shoulders, attempting to get him to touch it, but he took his time. Letting go of her breasts, he traced a pattern down the center of her body to her belly button.

His light touch sent ripples all over her body. She scissored her legs underneath him and tried to arch her hips into his, but he kept his just out of her reach.

"Antonio…"

"Sí, querida?"

"I need more," she said.

"You will get it but not as quickly as a star falls from the sky. This is more of the slow journey of a comet that orbits the sun and travels from the farthest reaches of the solar system."

His words made her heart beat faster and every nerve ending in her go on high alert. She liked making love with Antonio because, like everything else he did, he was thorough.

He lowered his head and nibbled at the skin of her belly, his tongue tracing the indentation of her belly button, and each time he dipped his tongue into her she felt her clit tingle. She shifted her hips to rub against him.

His mouth moved lower on her, his hands reaching the waistband of her jeans, undoing the button and slowly lowering the zipper. She felt the warmth of his breath on her lower belly and then the edge of his tongue as he traced the skin revealed by the opening.

"Lift your hips," he said.

She planted her feet on the blanket to comply. He tugged her jeans down over her hips, moving backward as he did so until the pant legs tangled with her boots.

Taking his time, he removed first one boot and then

the other before he got her jeans completely off. He sat back on his heels and lifted her left foot and drew it to one side until her legs were widely parted. He moved back up between her legs and palmed her through her panties, and she squirmed on the blanket. She wanted more.

He gave it to her, his hand on her most intimate flesh, and he drew her underwear down with his teeth. His hands kept moving over her stomach and thighs until she was completely naked and bare underneath him. Then he leaned back on his knees and just stared down at her.

"Every time we make love I want to make it last longer than the time before," he said in his heavily accented voice.

"Me, too. But then when I see you…when you touch me. It can't go fast enough," she said.

He shifted and moved forward again, touching her and caressing her, brushing his lips over her body. "But you also make me want to get inside you as quickly as I can and take you until we both go up in flames."

He spoke against her skin so that she felt the words all the way through her body. He lowered his head again and rubbed his chin over her mound, a back-and-forth motion that made her feel full and, at the same time, empty.

He parted her with the thumb and forefinger of his left hand, and she felt the air against her most intimate flesh and then the brush of his tongue. It was so soft and wet and she squirmed, wanting—no needing—more from him.

He scraped his teeth over her and she almost came right then, but he lifted his head and smiled up at her. Making her acknowledge once again that Antonio was the kind of lover who wanted to draw out the experience.

She gripped his shoulders as he teased her with his mouth, pushing her fingers into his hair and holding him close to her. He moaned against her and the sound tickled her, sending shivers racing up her spine and to the tips of her breasts.

He traced the opening of her body with one large, blunt finger, making her shift her hips and try to get him inside her. Her breasts felt full and her nipples were tight as he pushed just the tip of his finger inside of her.

The first ripples of her orgasm started to pulse through her.

"Antonio…"

"Yes?" he asked, lightly stroking her lower belly and then moving both hands to her breasts where he cupped the full globes.

"I need more."

"You will get it," he said.

She reached between their bodies and stroked him through his pants. She slowly lowered the tab of the zipper, but he caught her wrist.

"Once you do that, it will be all over," he said. "I have no control when you touch me."

"Good," she said, twisting her wrist to free his grip on her hand and undoing his zipper.

He lowered his body over hers so the soft fabric of his shirt brushed her breasts and stomach before she felt the masculine hardness of his muscles underneath. Then his thigh was between her legs moving slowly against her, and she moaned out loud as everything in her tightened just a little bit more.

But it wasn't enough. She undulated against him so that the sensations were even more intense than before. He moved again and she felt the warmth of his breath against her mound. She opened her eyes and saw the comet flashing through the sky, but she couldn't process it because his mouth was on her.

Each sweep of his tongue against her drove her higher and higher as everything in her body tightened, waiting for the touch that would push her over the edge. She shifted her legs around his head, felt the brush of his silky smooth hair against her inner thighs.

Her hips jerked forward and her nipples tightened. She felt the moisture between her legs and his finger pushing hard against her G-spot. She was shivering and her entire body was convulsing, but he didn't lift his head. He kept suckling on her and driving her harder and harder until she came again, screaming with her orgasm as stars danced behind her eyelids.

It was more than she could process and she had to close her eyes. She reached for Antonio, needing some sort of comfort after that storm of pleasure, and he was right there. He drew his hips back and entered her body, driving into her and making her orgasm last and last. He plunged into her again and again until he groaned her name and came inside her.

She held him close, watching the stars in the night sky and stroking her hands up and down his back as he rested his face in the curve of her neck. Tonight their lovemaking felt deeper, had touched her all the way to her soul.

Always after they had sex she had felt exposed and raw, but this time she didn't feel the need to retreat. She held on to Antonio, knowing he wasn't perfect and didn't expect her to be.

She held on to him, hoping that she would never have to let him go.

14

EVERYONE ON HER team was dressed in jeans, matching red plaid cowboy shirts that someone had ordered for them, straw cowboy hats and boots. They were all being transported out to the area of the ranch that the Bar T crew had set up for a rodeo. It was past the lake on part of the property that was closer to the Mick Tanner Training Facility. There were all-terrain four-wheelers that had some secondary trailers with built-in benches because the Memorial Day rodeo at the Bar T was a local event.

The cowboys from all of the local ranches came to compete against one another. The dummy steer-roping competition was usually something for the kids, and the Cronus candidates were participating because it was an event that was the least dangerous to them. Izzy had to admit she was excited. She hadn't slept at all once she and Antonio had gotten back from watching the stars. To be fair, the excitement could also be just exhaustion, since they had returned to their rooms at about three in the morning, having fallen asleep in each other's arms, and it was now eight o'clock.

"I can't believe we are going to a rodeo," Vicki Crum said. She'd joined the training program at the same time Izzy had and was currently dating one of the ranch hands. Izzy wasn't sure if that was okay with the commander.

"Me, neither. I'm pretty excited," Izzy said. "The only one I've ever been to is the PBR in Vegas. But that's a big-time event with lots of sponsors and a lot of show."

"It should be fun. Griffin is excited he's doing a steer-roping event. You know how we have to rope the steer? Well, with a real animal, it then has to be brought down. Takes a lot of strength. I'm a little bit scared for him," Vicki said.

Her friend did seem nervous. She was talking a lot more than she usually did. "I think it's way worse to worry about someone else than yourself. You know?"

"I do know. I called my mom last night and talked her ear off about it. She was funny and said that now I know how she feels every time I go to Russia for a liftoff to the ISS."

Izzy laughed. "That's funny. The rockets are perfectly safe and not unpredictable like a live animal."

"That's exactly what I said. Parents worry about the craziest things."

"They do," Izzy agreed, though her mom was less of a worrier than some. She knew that she'd raised her daughter to stand up to anything, so she didn't have to worry about her. Something that Izzy was very grateful for.

They all piled onto the vehicle and it took them out to the rodeo area. A temporary arena had been set up with bleachers on three of the sides. There were small pens at the far end of the arena where there were trucks and trailers parked, and neighboring ranchers getting their animals into pens and ready for the day. The bleachers weren't full, but a few people had already come to watch, and Rina had set up a food stand with lemonade, iced tea and snacks.

Ace waved. "Blue team, you're the first to arrive. Your event is going to be during the first break after the barrel riders. And I'd like everyone from our group to sit in those bleachers over there." He gestured to the third set of bleachers. Like them, he was dressed more like a cowboy than an astronaut.

"Hemi is running late, but he will be here before the event. He had to make an airport run to pick up his parents. Some of the neighboring ranchers have set up booths with crafts and stuff along the back of those bleachers. There will be an announcement when you need to take your seats. Any questions?" Ace asked.

"Is there a practice steer in case we want to warm up?" Izzy asked.

"Yeah," Ace said. "Over behind your bleachers. I think a few of the red team are already there. You guys need anything else?" Ace asked.

"Nah, I think we got it," Izzy said, glancing at the rest of her team.

When Ace walked away she turned to the group. "I

think we are free to wander around until the announcement that the event is starting. Then we can meet at our assigned seats. Does anyone want to get in some extra practice?" Izzy asked. She knew she wouldn't try it this morning, since yesterday she'd spent some time in the barn practicing and she didn't want to mess with her headspace.

"I could use some practice," Dean Winters said.

"Me, too," Meredith said. "But you don't need to come with us, Izzy."

"Okay, if you're sure," Izzy said.

"We are. Go enjoy the rodeo. I think even the team leader should get to have some downtime," Dean said.

"Then I'll see you all in a little bit," Izzy said, waving to Meredith and Dean as they moved off. Vicki fell into step besides Izzy and the two of them chatted as they looked at the different crafts that the ranchers had for sale.

Izzy was drawn to an etched-wood painting of a cowboy looking up at a night sky. For some reason it reminded her of Antonio. She lifted it up and realized that it had a fixture behind it for a light so that the sky could glow.

Loving it, she decided to buy it and asked the woman who'd made it to wrap it up for her.

Vicki bought a leather belt and they both purchased some lavender hand cream that was made locally before they walked over to the bleachers to watch the rodeo getting set up.

When she saw Antonio arrive with the rest of his team, she realized she'd been waiting for him. She let out a breath and some of her nerves calmed down. She was beginning to rely too much on him. But for today she wasn't going to worry about that.

ANTONIO UNDERSTOOD NOW why Dennis had been arguing against anyone in the training program hooking up. He was tired. He was definitely not at his best today, and he gave himself only the tiniest break by acknowledging that since this event was more fun competition than something they would be graded on, it was okay to be tired.

But that was how addiction had taken hold of his life a long time ago. He knew that once he started making excuses, it was damned hard to stop making them. And then he'd be staying out late with Izzy all the time because she made him feel so good.

Not that there was anything wrong with feeling good. But he knew he had to watch himself. Had to balance his pursuit of her with his focus on the mission and the spot that he wanted. That they both wanted.

And that was the truth. He wanted Izzy, of course, but he also wanted Cronus. Their talk last night had reminded him that he hadn't hit rock bottom and clawed his way back to the top of his field for nothing. And love was powerful, he knew that. He'd seen the example of his parents' marriage, but he'd also had seen the destructive side of it with his own destructive relationships.

He rubbed the back of his neck as Ace came over and told them all where they needed to be. Ace invited them to look around the area at the booths and he had that déjà vu feeling he got when he was on the Bar T sometimes. Like he could easily be back home at his parents' ranch. Even the sounds of the conversations, some of them in Spanish, served to further that illusion. He walked by the booths and thought about the present he'd purchased for Izzy.

He had meant to give it to her last night when they'd returned from their date, but it had been late and too much had happened. If Izzy had been the one to back away before, now it was him backing away. But he knew that was all down to letting her in too close. He should have realized with Izzy he'd never be able to keep his walls up where they needed to be.

Honestly, she was the worst sort of addiction for him, and he was concerned that he was going to have to break it off with her. The problem was, he wasn't sure he could. He walked past the different craft tables and stopped to buy a charm from a silversmith that was an Aztec-style sun for his mom. He also purchased a leather necklace for the charm and then slipped it into his pocket.

Even when he thought about their teams, it was more thinking about Izzy than about besting her. Not that winning meant they'd be selected for the first mission. There was a mix of things that Ace, Thor and Dennis were looking for in the candidates. And Antonio knew he had a pretty good mix of most of them.

He wanted Izzy, but it was more than the physical, though each time they made love he wanted her even more than he had before. A part of him wanted to believe that there was no reason he should crave her that badly but, honestly, just seeing her sitting with the blue team on the benches made him start to harden.

He wanted her.

He needed her.

He resented that feeling. Not the woman. Not Izzy. It wasn't her fault he had an addictive personality and was falling for possibly the right woman at the wrong time.

She did feel like the right woman. She made him stronger most of the time; it was only now when he needed to be calm and focused that he was starting to wonder if he ever would be with her by his side. He would use today as a test. If he could get through the event and perform at his highest level, then he'd know that he could handle Izzy and the pressure of the job.

If not, then he should recuse himself from the running for the first crew. He was pretty sure that he and Izzy wouldn't both be chosen, but he needed to be sure that they could work together. That he wasn't going to become so besotted with her he couldn't do his job.

Having made up his mind, he already felt more confident. There had been few things in this world that he had wanted with this much intensity. One was space and his dream of being part of the team that would work toward the first large, long-term habitable space station away from earth's orbit. The second was booze. It would be a lie to say that he hadn't wanted it, and sometimes still did. But he had ways of coping with that, taking Arabella out for a ride and now of course he had Carly, his sweet little dog, had helped there because in the middle of the night he could take her for a walk. She needed him so he couldn't screw up.

The last was Izzy.

He had wanted to somehow make his attraction to her into a sexual thing or a competitive thing only. But it never had been. Even from the beginning he'd suspected that it wasn't, and now he had to admit to himself that he was falling for her.

For the first time in a very long while he actually felt he was on the cusp of having it all. *Or.* Or losing everything that he'd worked so hard to bring into his life—and that included Izzy.

THE RODEO WAS fun despite the hot weather. Everyone was flagging a little bit as they sat on the bleachers, but once they were all up on their feet and loosening up for their event, spirits rose.

"Now we have a treat for you," the announcer said. "As many of you know, part of the Bar T has been leased by the space program and we have some real-life genuine astronauts with us today. These men and women are going to help take us to Mars and beyond, and we couldn't be prouder to call them part of our community."

There was a round of applause. Izzy noticed most of the candidates, including Antonio, looked a little embarrassed by the buildup in the announcement, but these were their jobs and pretty cool ones, at that.

"I just feel lucky that I get to do this," Dean said.

"Amen, brother," Izzy said.

"The candidates will be competing in two teams, red and blue. Keep in mind most of these greenhorns haven't done much ranching or cowboying in their lives, but I saw them practicing earlier and they are pretty decent. So please, ladies and gentlemen, put your hands together for the Cronus red and Cronus blue dummy steer-roping teams."

Someone played the theme song from *The Right Stuff* as they all walked out into the arena. Two dummy steers awaited them, sawhorses rigged with a bale of hay that had a pair of Texas longhorn horns wedged into the front.

"Good luck," Antonio said.

"Same to you," Izzy said. "But I don't think I'm going to need luck. I'm pretty good at this."

He looked tired and, to her eyes, maybe a little worried. "Remember last night? I've done this before, too."

She waited half a beat and then winked at him as her team was called. "I don't think being good at sex is going to help you."

She followed her other team members to their mark in front of one of the dummy steers and heard Antonio's bark of laughter. She smiled to herself. She had to keep reminding herself that every time she became really good at something, be it school or engineering or whatever, she had been relaxed. She'd never won when she was thinking she had to win.

Her team had already discussed the lineup, but as they noticed the way the red team was staggered, with Antonio in the front going first, Meredith gestured for everyone to gather close.

"I think Antonio is the best on their team. He's like Izzy, trained to catch things in space and draw them to the space station. Should we change our order?" Meredith asked.

"I don't think it matters. They are going to record our time and number of attempts," Dean said.

"We just all have to do our best," Izzy said. "We've got this, guys. We have all practiced and our skills are pretty good. If you feel that moving the order around will help, then we will do it. But there isn't a one of us who can't do this."

"Thanks for reminding us, Izzy. I'm ready to kick some butt," Meredith said.

Antonio did, indeed, go first and set a pretty impressive time, getting the steer on his first attempt. As the teams cycled through, they teased one another, but applauded each success. In the end it was Izzy's team who won but by the narrowest of margins, and it drove home to her just how the level of training was for this mission.

She also realized that Ace and Dennis were building in redundancies even in the team. Now everyone could use the crane to capture an object in space. That was smart thinking. She knew that she'd been scheduled for classes that weren't her area of expertise, as well. Everyone was going to have enough knowledge to fill in for each other once they were in space.

"Congratulations, *querida*," Antonio said, coming up to her after everyone had filed back out of the arena.

"Thank you, babe," she said, with a wink. "I wasn't too sure we were going to be able to beat you guys. Everyone is really good at this, aren't they?"

He nodded. "There isn't a person on my team that

wants to be a member of the B team. Everyone wants to make that first mission."

"Same. The competition is fierce. I'm proud to be a part of this," she said.

"Me, too," Antonio said. "Listen, I have something for you."

She tipped her head to the side to study him. "I have something for you, too."

"I guess that proves we are thinking along the same lines."

"Does it?" she asked. She thought it proved that she was starting to fall for her space cowboy. A man who was strong and smart and had hidden weaknesses that he was overcoming every day.

She had to admit the weaknesses made her care even more for him. It had been hard to think of living up to the perfection she'd seen in Antonio, but now she knew he wasn't flawless. He was human just like her. She looked up and noticed that he was staring down at the light she'd gotten for him, tracing the etched wood.

And she knew that she wasn't falling for him. She had fallen. Hard.

15

THE MEMORIAL DAY weekend saw a shift in the way the teams were treated. Each team had completed time in the simulator on their own to allow each of the specialists time to get comfortable in the surroundings. But now they had to check all of the variables of personalities and team dynamics.

It was the second week in June and everyone was exhausted. Izzy had never seen the astronauts in such good shape and also so anxious. Everyone was honed to the razor's edge, including herself. Though she and Antonio had been spending their downtime together, the amount of time available to them was becoming less and less.

She missed him.

It was silly. She was physically in the same space as he was at least ten hours a day, but they were so busy, everyone doing their own tasks, that there was no time to talk or bond. Today they were going back into the simulator. They had been working on assembling the first part of the space station in the large indoor pool that had been specifically designed for them and held the prototype shuttle vehicle. Yesterday had been particularly long because the first piece of the way station was bigger than anything any of them had tried before to assemble in the space environment.

"I don't understand why it works in virtual reality," Izzy said to Antonio as they were suiting up for the underwater extravehicular simulations that they would be working on today.

"Me, neither," Antonio said. "Last night when I got back to my room, I ran through the virtual program again, and nearest I can tell is that possibly there is a variable written into the algorithm that we don't know about."

"That's what I was thinking. I'm not sure if that is something deliberate to ensure that we don't get too complacent in thinking that because we could do it on the computer it will be easy in space," Izzy said. It was the only option that made any sense to her.

She looked around the locker room where everyone was suiting up and talking quietly in pairs like she and Antonio were, or rereading manuals. She reached over and touched Antonio's shoulder. Gave him a little squeeze.

He turned and dropped a kiss on her hand. Which made her feel so much better about the two of them. They'd had a fight yesterday in the control room about what needed to be done about the order of operations, and she hadn't been able to tell him afterward that she wasn't mad at him personally. It was just the job.

The door opened and Hemi walked in, followed by Ace. Everyone stopped what they were doing to look at the only two men who knew they were going on the first Cronus mission.

"Good morning," Ace said. "We are going to be joining you in the simulator today and in the water."

"Why now?" Velosi asked. "Is it because of our failure to stay on track yesterday?"

"Not at all," Hemi said. "It is because we realized that there is something different in the practical than all of the virtual test runs, and as we are going to be working together as team, it made no sense for us to be in the booth."

"Plus, Thor was jealous. He wants a chance to be in the thick of it with all of you," Ace said.

"I was," Hemi said, putting his hands on his hips. "We want to make today's exercise as real as possible. So Ace will be in the command module with myself, Meredith and Hennessey. The rest of you are experts on building and assembling and we are going to let you all work together."

"Great. One of the options I thought about last night was that we might need more hands than we initially thought," Izzy said.

"I agree," Antonio added. "The left section seems to be off balance. Possibly due to the space dock. We might have to break it down."

The other candidates added their ideas, and Hemi and Ace listened and then drew the group over to a large whiteboard at the end of the locker room. Ace sketched the docking piece that was giving them all such a hard time and everyone took turns adding ideas to the board, trying different combinations of staff inside the space shuttle and outside of it.

As they worked side by side, Izzy, Antonio, Velosi and Vicki seemed to be driving the ideas, and since they had been working with everyone on the teams every day, they knew who would work well together. Izzy realized that instead of taking away from her ability to do her job, working with Antonio was making her stronger. She was used to hearing his thoughts from the hours they'd spent talking and going over things, so their minds ran along the same paths.

"I think we have the beginnings of a very workable plan. We will all go onto the space shuttle and then deploy outside the vehicle one by one and start work," Ace said. "Dennis is here observing, as is Mal from Space Now and Jose Velasquez from the international space program. They are anxious to see us in action. Let's not disappoint them."

"That's really why you are in here with us, isn't it?" Velosi asked. "They want to see us all in action."

"Yes, they do, and rightfully so," Ace said. "They deserve the chance to see what we can do and how we are progressing. To be fair, the video updates that they have been receiving have everyone very excited and that is why they are here. You are a very impressive group," Ace said.

"Everyone, gather your stuff and let's go," Hemi said.

"Ready to be impressive?" Antonio asked.

"You bet," Izzy said. "Let's show them that they have everything they need in our teams."

The excitement in the group was palpable. They'd been working for the last six weeks for this moment.

THE FIRST THING Antonio noticed when they were all off the shuttle and moving into position was that everyone was paying close attention to every detail. He wondered if it would have been better if Ace hadn't talked to them about being observed by the people who were in charge of the mission. The candidates were very aware that today they had to get the dock assembled.

"Everyone looks nervous, but also ready to go," Izzy said.

"I think there is added pressure today," Velosi said. "I know I'm feeling it."

"Me, too," Antonio added. "We need to do something to break the tension or we are all going to be too on edge to deal with assembling the dock."

"Agreed," Velosi said. "Anyone got any ideas?"

Izzy shook her head. "The team is so diverse, and everyone responds to different types of motivators."

"Guys," Antonio said abruptly. "Can we have a minute?"

The blended teams all turned toward them and he saw his own feelings reflected in the faces of the people he'd come to know over the last six weeks. They all wanted this—badly. They had all worked their entire lives to be here and they needed the Cronus mission program to continue and to not have any more delays. Some of the astronauts had been waiting too long for an opportunity like this.

"Sure, Playboy, what's up?"

Antonio rubbed the back of his neck and then cleared his throat. He thought of the things that he feared most in the world and knew they weren't here in the command module or out there in the simulated space environment.

Everyone wore the white suits that were modern versions of the iconic space suits that the original astronauts wore for the Apollo missions. Their spot in history suddenly felt very real to him as he looked at the men and women he knew so well.

"Don't forget we are standing in the footsteps of giants," Antonio said. "We are the product of everyone who has made it their goal to leave this planet and explore space. And today we are going to take it one step further."

"Playboy is right. We are the best of the best, and there is no reason for us to doubt ourselves," Izzy added.

"Over the last few weeks we've all had the chance to observe each other in action. We are the best—as evidenced by our coming up with the new plan of action," Velosi added.

"I just wanted to say thank you to everyone. We've worked really hard and become a family, not just a team. And one thing I know about family is that you always have each other's back. I wanted to say that no matter what happens out there today, we were chosen for this and we shouldn't forget it." He had started rambling, and it was only when Izzy put her hand on his forearm that he stopped talking.

"I agree. I get the feeling that Ace and Thor were just as surprised by our visitors as we were," she said.

"But we all know if they are here it's because they've heard that we are getting close to being mission ready."

"Hell, we are already mission ready," Velosi said. "Let's blow their expectations out of the water and show them what multinational cooperation really looks like. No politics or teams competing, just astronauts doing what we were trained for."

"What we've dreamed about for the longest time," Antonio added. "No matter what happens today, everyone only has to do their job."

"We got this," Izzy added.

"Yeah, we do."

There were cheers from all of the candidates. Antonio looked at Izzy and Velosi, knowing that the three of them worked really well together. The teams would too today.

Everyone finished suiting up and checked their oxygen tanks, and Antonio pulled Izzy aside. He leaned in and kissed her. "I'm glad that we are both here. And no matter who wins today, who earns those three remaining spots on the first mission, I don't want our relationship to end."

"Now? Seriously, we can't think about each other right now," she said.

"I can. You make me stronger," he said. "With you by my side I know I can do anything. Sorry if I distracted you."

"You didn't," she said. "I just... Never mind—we can talk later."

Antonio nodded, but he felt her pulling away from him. No matter what she'd said earlier, there was some part of Izzy that needed to do this by herself. To prove to herself and the world that she didn't need anyone.

How had he missed that before this? How had he not noticed that while he'd been letting himself fall in love with her, she'd been managing to figure out how to prove that she could still be independent?

It bothered him, and he had to shake his head to clear it. She was right—he shouldn't have pulled her aside to talk. He should have stayed focused on the mission.

He felt someone watching him and looked up to see Hemi staring from across the room. Antonio hoped he hadn't just screwed up and taken himself out of the running.

But the truth was that he and Izzy were a couple. Everyone knew it, and her acting like they were just teammates today unnerved him. Everything in his relationship with her was harder than he'd expected it to be.

He'd talk to her tonight and they'd get this sorted out. Today he had to make sure he and his team performed the way they all knew they could.

The first underwater session went flawlessly. Everyone was pumped and the nerves that had been present in the locker room had dissipated once they were in the water and working together.

They had finally gotten the first piece into place, but it had taken three more astronauts than everyone had originally thought it would. But since this was a new environment and something no one had done before,

Izzy guessed that the director wasn't going to be disappointed that they needed more staff.

With so many different agencies working together, it seemed to her that they would be able to come up with the additional funding. Everyone reentered the main shuttle for a lunch break. Because they were under water but on the station they had the simulated artificial gravity working. The corridors were small for so many people, and the eating area had been designed for eight people at most. So it was uncomfortable as they crowded in there and were handed rations.

Everyone talked about what had just been done and the next steps they would take when they went back out into the water. Antonio was seated with a few of the people from Space Now, and Izzy knew she'd hurt him when she'd brushed him off earlier.

She might make him stronger, but she wasn't sure he did the same for her. When they were out there working, she hadn't been distracted by him. She'd known she could count on Antonio to be where he was supposed to be and to do what was needed to get the job done.

She knew they had to talk. She had expected some kind of announcement about couples on the mission soon. There were a few other couples in their group, but everyone was ready to accept whatever Dennis and the powers that be stated. If couples weren't allowed on missions together, they would do what they had always done. Go back to the single, solitary lives.

It wasn't really that big of a deal.

Except that Izzy realized she wanted Antonio to make the first mission almost as much, if not more, than she wanted it for herself. She thought of how hard they had both worked to get here and she realized that she didn't want anything to keep them from achieving their goal...together.

Velosi came into the room with his suit on and a look on his face that she'd never seen before. And she'd known the man for a long time.

"Let's go. Something is wrong with the dock and it's listing. It looks like it might hit the simulator."

Everyone dropped their food and started suiting up. The process was meant to take at least fifteen minutes but everyone seemed to be double-checking each other so they could get out in the pool more quickly.

She ended up next to Antonio and they checked each other's tanks.

"Turn around," she said, noticing that his was low and reaching for a replacement one. "You only have half a tank of oxygen."

He did as she asked and she changed out his tank. They were the second to last people to leave the shuttle, but safety had to come first and Izzy wasn't bothered by that.

As they exited the shuttle, a loud explosion ripped through the air. Antonio grabbed Izzy's hand as waves rippled through the pool and they were propelled backward, spinning and spinning. Izzy felt the first panic she'd experienced in a long time. She closed her eyes and when she opened them she saw Antonio next to her.

"You okay?" he asked, using the radio in his helmet that linked them all together.

"Yes, you?" she responded.

"Yes," Antonio said.

"This is Bombshell. Everyone report in. Just call signs so we know you are okay," Izzy said after flicking a switch to broadcast to everyone.

After the call signs had poured in, she realized that Velosi hadn't reported in.

"Where is Velocity?" Izzy asked. "Does anyone have eyes on him?"

"I just caught sight of him. He's drifting toward the bottom of the pool," Hennessey said. "He's pinned under a piece of the dock."

"Red team, we've got the dock," Antonio said. "Blue team, get Velocity."

"On it. Blue team switch to B channel so that we aren't interfering with Red."

Izzy squeezed Antonio's hand before she used the built-in mechanical engine to propel herself to the rest of her team. They were all doing the same thing. Their suits were meant for space, so there wasn't an easy way to swim down to Velosi. They had to use the suits to descend, which Izzy hoped wouldn't take up precious time.

"Velocity, we are on our way to you."

"Hurry up, Bombshell," Velosi said, sounding winded. "I'm trapped."

"Whoever reaches Velocity first, assess his medical condition and, if we need to, we will free him from the suit and take him to the surface," Izzy said.

"Bombshell, I'm with him and he is wedged. His leg is under the structure."

"Copy that. I'm switching channels to relay the

information to the red team. Frosty, you're in command," Izzy said. Dean Winters was very reliable and she trusted him.

She switched channels.

"Playboy, come in."

"Go ahead."

"Velocity's leg is wedged underneath the platform we just installed. We can't free him unless we move it," she said.

"Got it. We are already working to shift the collapsed part of the dock. We should have it free in about ten—"

Antonio was cut off by another rumble. More waves ripped through the pool. Izzy went tumbling again and looked up to where Antonio had been and only saw a cloud of rubble.

"Playboy, come in?"

Nothing but silence. She switched to the B channel. "Team report."

"We're all good—we were able to hang on to Velocity."

"Got it, everyone switch to A."

"Playboy?" she asked. Despite the lump in her throat, she'd continue to do her job. But she needed to know that Antonio was okay.

16

ANTONIO HAD ONE of the other astronauts by the arm; she'd been hit by some of the debris as the platform continued to collapse. He heard the worry in Izzy's voice but was glad she was okay. He propelled himself and Meredith toward the surface.

"I'm here. Sorry. Meredith was hit in the last collapse and I am taking her to the surface. I'll be back in a moment. Bomber, take over command of the red team. And let's get everyone out of the pool."

"Yes, sir," Bomber said. "Bombshell, where is your team?"

"Still with Velocity. Anyone else who was injured?"

There were a series of nos, which made Antonio feel better. He got Meredith to the surface where Doc Tomlin waited. He handed Meredith to her and then used his suit to propel himself back under the surface.

Everyone worked together to disassemble and shift what was left of the dock off Velocity.

"What's the status on Velocity?" Antonio asked.

"Still wedged. But I think if we shift the long arm piece out of the way we should be able to free him," Izzy said.

Antonio found himself working next to her and watching the dock as they worked. They'd been careful in assembling the pieces earlier and it was taking precious time to get everything broken apart enough to free the trapped man. Time that Antonio could see they were running out of.

"Playboy, I'm getting a low-oxygen warning," Hennessey said. "I'm down here with Velocity. Can someone take over?"

Hell. This situation was going from bad to worse.

"I can," Antonio said. He had a new tank thanks to Izzy. He started his descent and as soon as he was there, Hennessey gave him the thumbs-up sign and ascended. From his new position he could see that Velocity was awake but looked possibly concussed. They needed to get him out of the pool.

Antonio moved toward Velocity's wedged leg and then had an idea, one that might not be approved and certainly couldn't be used in space, but they were in the pool and Velosi needed out now.

"Izzy, how's your oxygen?"

"Good, why?"

"I want to try to cut Velocity free. But once I cut his suit, it's going to let water in. I need someone to help me pull him free of the structure.

"One minute. Anyone who has enough oxygen, go to the bottom of the pool."

Four team members, along with Izzy, were able to get to Velocity.

"This is what I'm thinking. His suit is wedged with part of his leg but I think if I cut his suit it might free him. I'm worried about the integrity breach of his suit, though. Water might go in. I need someone who can do rescue breathing with him," Antonio said.

"I got the rescue breathing," Hemi said, coming on the communication link.

"Thor?"

"Hell, yes. The emergency folks are on their way, but right now we are the ones who have to get him out. Ace has the crane and is ready to lift most of this when we tell him," Thor said. "I like your plan, Playboy. How stable is the base?"

"I don't have a clear view of it," Antonio said.

"It's wedged," Izzy said. "It's like something drove it down into the bottom of the pool."

"Okay. So shifting it isn't going to happen unless Ace can get it with the crane. Is he on the same comms as we are?" Thor asked.

"I'm here. Sorry for the delay," Ace said. "Is the structure stable enough for me to grab it or is it going to collapse again?"

"It's hard to tell," Antonio answered. "Based on how it keeps shifting apart, I'd say no. But if you could grab the top and pull it upward while we lift the bottom we might be able to free him."

"Anyone have an objection to Playboy's plan?"

There were a series of negative answers. Antonio felt the pressure to get this right.

"Playboy, you're in charge," Ace said.

Thor took over with Velosi, and Antonio moved to the base where it was wedged on Velosi's leg. He knew his knife would work to free the fabric, but as he got closer he could see that it Velosi's boot was also trapped.

That mean this foot was probably stuck under the structure, as well. With Izzy and Hennessey next to him, Antonio took the lead.

He handed his knife to Izzy and then turned to Hennessey.

"We might be able to lift this if we plant our feet on the bottom. But we're going to have to keep the mechanical engine on for resistance against the ground. Can we get an assist from Vicki and Barney?"

"Yes."

"I see what you mean. I'll take the left," Hennessey said.

"Izzy, you cut first to free his suit and then we will lift while you pull."

"Got it," Izzy said.

Vicki went to Hennessey, and Barney came over to him. Antonio would have to keep one hand free so that Barney would be able to keep the pressure on the engine to keep him grounded on the bottom. But it should work.

"On my count," Izzy said. "Three. Two. One. Making the cut now."

Antonio watched Izzy working and knew that the structure was unstable. He worried it might fall on her and knew he'd sacrifice himself for her if that happened. He'd do whatever he had to in order to make sure she was safe.

"Okay done. Thor, ready?"

"Ready."

"Three, two, one."

He and Hennessey both shoved at the structure and it budged and then toppled as Izzy and Thor pulled Velosi free. Barney let go of his hand. Vicki got behind to make sure that Velosi was able to move.

"Start ascending," Thor ordered. "He's free."

They all started the ascent and as they broke the surface, Antonio saw many people on the deck, including emergency services, but he couldn't find Izzy.

WHEN VELOCITY WAS freed, Izzy looked around to make sure that everyone was safely on their way up, and as she did, a part of the structure fell straight toward her. There was another of those ripples that jostled her balance, knocking her hand off her motor and making her lose control over her movement.

She tumbled head over heels in a disorienting roll that left her unsure which way was up. She had a moment where she felt completely alone and lost.

She had been in control up until this moment, but she couldn't do this alone. She hated that feeling. And she was afraid for a second. Then she heard Antonio's voice in her ear.

"Izzy? Where are you?"

There was a sense of calm in his tone. "I'm still in the water. I got jostled when the structure moved."

"Are you okay?"

"Yes. Just need to figure out which way is up," she said, turning in a circle. Seeing the lights from the shuttle, she realized which way she needed to head. She started moving again, finding her bearings.

"Figured it out. I'm on my way up," she said. The difference of being in the pool and being in space was palpable. While the water made her feel like she did when on a space walk, it was thicker and it was harder to move through water than it was through space.

If something like this had happened when they were on a mission, she could have been lost. But she wasn't.

When she surfaced, she looked around for Antonio and saw that one of the medical technicians was holding his arm to keep him from going back in the water. She couldn't help smiling at that. If there was one thing she knew, it was that Antonio was never going to leave her behind.

And suddenly she knew she loved him.

Oh. My. God.

It was true.

She loved Antonio.

The man who'd been her biggest competitor.

The man who made her crazy and turned her on.

She loved him.

After a lifetime of keeping men at arm's length and of always having to do everything for herself, she'd found the person who would stay with her. No matter what. That moment of clarity was easier to take now that the emergency was over. They'd survived what could have been a horrible disaster. One of the EMTs came and pulled her out of the water. She wanted to ask about Velosi, but she couldn't take her eyes off Antonio.

He'd settled down as soon as he saw her. She gave him the thumbs-up and he nodded at her. She answered the questions the EMT asked her.

"Do you know how Velosi is? He looked concussed," Izzy said to the EMT.

"They transported him to the hospital. I can't comment on his health officially, but he looked like he was feeling better when they loaded him on the medevac helicopter."

"Thanks," she said. "Was anyone else injured?"

"Nope, the rest of you seem to be checking out okay," he said. "Once I'm done monitoring your blood-oxygen level you will be cleared to go with your team."

"Thank you," she said again. She leaned back against the wall and closed her eyes as he hooked the monitor up to her middle finger.

"You okay, Bombshell?" Ace asked as he sat down next to her.

"Yeah. I think I am. What the hell happened?" she asked. "Was this one of your tests?" she asked. She hoped it hadn't been, because it was dangerous. They were all trained in the pool, but that collapse had been... more than anyone had expected. It was the kind of accident that could have had a much more disastrous effect.

"Not a test. I was as shocked as you were when it collapsed. Dennis is in a room with Mal and Jose trying to figure out what the hell happened. You were good under pressure," he said.

"Everyone was," Izzy said. "If you needed proof that we can all function as a team, I'd say you have it."

"True. It was hard to be in the shuttle and watch everything unfold. I'm glad we were able to get Velosi out," Ace said. "I'm going to have a debriefing as soon as everyone is cleared from medical. And I know Doc Tomlin wants to run some tests."

"Makes sense. Were you recording in the pool while we were in the shuttle?" she asked.

"Affirmative. The cameras are always on when we have people in the simulator," Ace said.

"That's good. Maybe we can see if the collapse had something to do with the equipment or if it was because of the way we assembled it."

"I don't think it was the assembly," Antonio said as he sat down next to her. He reached for her free hand and she laced their fingers together. She didn't hear what Ace said next because she was staring into Antonio's dark eyes, overwhelmed by the sense of relief she felt now that they were both safe.

"I don't, either. We ran the new assembly plan through the virtual simulator while you all were working and there were no problems with it," Ace said. "But we can discuss that at the debriefing. You two were a very effective team. Everyone respects you."

"Thanks, Ace," Antonio said. Izzy just had her head back against the wall and watched him. "We have a really great team here."

"Yes, we do."

Ace walked away, and a few minutes later the tech

removed the monitor from her finger. "You're clear. Nice job."

Antonio shifted so he was next to her with his back against the wall and put his arm around her shoulder. She wanted to turn into the curve of his body and hug him to her, but she was very aware that there were others watching them.

She didn't mind if Antonio saw her when she was weak, but she didn't want anyone else to. He was the only man she trusted to see her that way.

ANTONIO HELPED IZZY to her feet. He wanted a private moment with her, but that wasn't going to happen for a while. He knew they were being observed, and he was pretty sure that whatever decision was made about couples going on the mission, the way they worked together today hadn't done anything to hurt their chances. The fact was everyone had worked well. No one had freaked out.

"I think today was a good day," Antonio said as they walked to the locker room. "I for one wouldn't mind being on a team with any of the candidates. That trial by fire proved our skills in a way nothing else could."

"You're right," Izzy said. "I asked Ace if this was another one of his tests and he said no. But, damn, if something like that happens when we are assembling the station, we definitely know we can handle it."

Antonio brushed a strand of her hair from her face. "I think I would have freaked out if anything had happened to you."

She looked around the area. Everyone was in various

stages of removing their suits and changing back into their khakis and mission shirts. Izzy took his hand and drew him into a corner, then wrapped her arms around him and went up on tiptoe to kiss him.

He was startled for a second and then hugged her tightly to him. He was never letting go. He angled his head and deepened his kiss. Into the kiss he poured everything that he felt. The love, the fear, the joy that they were both alive. He lifted his head, framing her face with his hands, taking a moment just to stare into her eyes.

"Good God, woman, you scared me when I couldn't get you on the comms."

"Same. I hated being separated from you. I kept my focus on the job, but if anything had happened to you… I don't know what I would have done."

"Me, neither," he said. "I need you. We have the meeting, and as soon as we are dismissed for the day, I'm taking you to my room so I can feel you with every inch of my body and reassure my soul that you are safe."

He knew he was revealing too much. She might not feel the same, but when the woman he loved had come so close to dying he couldn't pull his punches. He realized that what he felt for Izzy wasn't at all like his dangerous addiction had been. It took hold of him, but it wasn't crippling. Nothing could tear them apart.

That made him scared. The only other times he'd felt this confident in anything and anyone had been his parents. He had never trusted anyone the way he was starting to trust Izzy.

"Yo, Bombshell and Playboy, time for that later, we need to get changed so we can debrief," Hennessey said.

Antonio pulled away as Izzy blushed. She pushed around him and gave Hennessey the finger as she went to her locker. Antonio did the same thing. Izzy had retreated behind her walls again. She wasn't comfortable yet with anyone else seeing them together.

Perhaps it wasn't just their schedule keeping them apart. Could it be that his secrets and his past had affected the way she looked at him? Did she see him as someone who could bring her down?

He couldn't answer those questions, but he did know one thing. Izzy and he were meant to be together, and if he had to keep coming back to her and wooing and winning her time and again, that was exactly what he'd do. He'd learned something when he couldn't raise her on the radio earlier.

And that was that he couldn't live without her in his life. He loved her, and that was strong enough to make him feel he could move mountains. Even if one of the mountains was Izzy herself.

He knew she had a good reason to keep her guard up all her life and he wasn't going to be one of those. He thought he'd already proved it, but it seemed there was still work to be done.

Damn.

He went into one of the private dressing rooms to get changed, and when he came out Izzy had gone. He joined the last of their group walking down the hall to the big meeting room. Hemi was waiting at the back with a checklist.

"That's it. You guys are the ones," Hemi said. "Grab a seat so we can get started."

Antonio took a spot at the back of the room, leaning against the wall noting that Izzy was sitting across the room. The briefing room was set up classroom-style with rows of chairs that faced a podium in the front.

Dennis entered the room, followed by Mal and Jose. Mal nodded at Antonio and he thought that at least he'd impressed his boss.

Maybe it wasn't the men that had always been leaving her and when she was child she'd had no control over it, but as an adult it seemed to him that she was very good at shoving men—well, him—out of her life. But he was determined to show her that she didn't have to run from him.

17

Izzy knew she'd run away from Antonio in the locker room, but he was getting too close. She wasn't ready to deal with her feelings directly, so she'd done the cowardly thing and snuck out while he'd been changing.

She was anxious to get out of this meeting and realized she had been feeling claustrophobic since the ascent in the gravity pool. She was more rattled than she wanted to admit. But when she closed her eyes, instead of Velosi pinned to the bottom of the pool she saw Antonio. She wasn't ready to admit how much that scared her.

Living with him was something she was just getting used to, and she didn't want to think about what it would be like to live without him.

Meredith was seated next to her, along with Vicki and Dean. Meredith was still shaken and freaked out a little bit by the fact that her oxygen tank had gotten so low. It wasn't equipment failure but rushing into an emergency without checking their equipment that had caused her failure.

Ace walked into the room to the podium and Izzy felt everyone come to attention. "Hello, Cronus candidates. I want to start by letting you know that Velosi is doing well and he will be back at the facility in a few days' time."

Everyone clapped and Izzy felt a sense of relief that her friend was okay. Ace waited for them to settle down and then looked at his notes before turning his attention back at them. He made eye contact with each of them and she wasn't sure what he was going to say next.

"The accident in the pool wasn't set up as a test, but, honestly, we couldn't have designed a better one. Though if it had been a test we would have had safety personnel on hand before we started. That being said, every single one of you preformed above average. Not one person thought of themselves first, and everyone focused on the job they were given and the overall mission at hand." Ace looked up from his notes and smiled at them. "Thank you for proving we chose the best."

Everyone smiled nervously. They knew this building up was leading to something. She suspected that it was the naming of crew members for the first mission.

"We have structural engineers from the company who built the platform on their way here to examine the structure, and they are going over the video that we took of today's events. Everyone has agreed that you all did nothing to cause the collapse and that the assembly process, while different from the original plan, doesn't seem to be the problem," Ace said. "I liked the way you brainstormed solutions with myself and Hemi this morning, and it was reassuring to me as the team leader to know that each person had something to contribute.

"We are going to be announcing the first mission crew tomorrow. I want you all to go home for the night, take some time off," Ace said. "The Bar T has invited everyone to dinner at the main house tonight. Are there any questions?"

"I have one."

Izzy turned to look at Antonio, who stood in the back leaning against the wall. He looked every inch the badass she knew he could be. This wasn't her lover she was seeing but a man who would stop at nothing to be named to the first Cronus mission.

"Go ahead," Ace said.

"I know there has been some discussion around the inclusion of couples on the missions. Has there been a decision about that?"

Everyone turned back to Ace, who shuffled the papers in front of him and rubbed the back of his neck before shaking his head. "We are assessing every candidate on their own. If we end up with two candidates who are also in a romantic relationship then we are going to have a discussion among ourselves and a separate one with the couple. This isn't something to be talked about in this forum."

Izzy didn't look back at Antonio, but she feared what Ace hadn't said. They weren't married. They were two people that had hooked up here in Cole's Hill. Would that be enough to convince the powers that be that the two of them were a solid couple and that if something did happen during the long, confined months they were on a mission, it wouldn't affect the entire crew.

"Are there any other questions?"

"Will we continue to train here or move to Houston?"

"The training will continue here once the teams are named. Everyone will have the option to live in Cole's Hill, and there are two new subdivisions being built to handle our staff. Temporarily, the bunkhouses will be used. But eventually we want the bunkhouses to just be for the new recruits, and anyone in a named mission will be able to have a normal home life in Cole's Hill."

"Anything else?"

"Are all of us going to be assigned to a mission?" Izzy asked.

Ace nodded. "Yes. We are going to name the first crew along with the crew for the second mission and back up crews for both. We are going to use the crew for the second mission as backup for the first and so on. You will be given your schedule and we are hopeful a launch date will be confirmed, as well. Any other questions?"

There was a round of applause and an air of excitement in the room.

There weren't any more questions and Ace left. Izzy stood and looked for Antonio, but he was already gone. She got stopped by and chatted with a few of her friends until she was finally able to head back to the bunkhouse. But when she got there she noticed that Antonio's pickup truck wasn't in the parking lot.

ANTONIO FED AND walked Carly and then, instead of going back to his room to spend the night waiting with the other candidates, he put his dog in the cab of his truck and headed for town. He needed to get away from everyone, especially Izzy.

His demons followed him, but they always did, and he found himself back at The Bull Pit. He parked in the lot and left the car running with the air-conditioning on. Just sat there thinking about Izzy. Carly came over and curled up next to him. He reached down and petted the dog, but his mind was on Izzy.

He wasn't a man who could hide anything about his life. He'd been up-front and honest from the beginning with her about that. His one secret really wasn't a secret if anyone dug hard to find it. But Izzy was all smoke and mirrors. She kept the real woman hidden, and he was beginning to think he was going to pay for having uncovered her.

Izzy wasn't the kind of woman to just let herself fall in love and be happy. She had to keep her walls in place. He wondered if she was still competing. Maybe trying to make him fall in love with her so she could win again.

He shook his head. He was just being a dick because he was angry. That wasn't the way Izzy was. He wished she were…almost. But he knew if she had been like that, he wouldn't have fallen for her. He heard the roar of a powerful engine and glanced to his left to see Izzy and her Mustang pulling to a stop next to his truck. She hopped out as soon as she turned the vehicle off.

She'd come after him…that had to mean something. She walked around to the passenger side of his truck and Carly was on her feet running over to the door as Izzy opened it. Carly licked Izzy's face and Izzy petted the dorgi before climbing up into the cab and closing the door behind her.

"I guess we're even now."

"How do you figure?" he asked, not sure where she was going with this.

"I left you in the locker room, you left me at the facility. We are going to have to stop doing this," she said. "Aren't we?"

"Are we?" he asked. He was tired of always being the one to put himself on the line first. He knew that wasn't the way a real gentleman would behave. His own father would kick his butt for being so vague, but then, his dad hadn't been in love with a woman like Isabelle Wolsten. Izzy wasn't the kind of woman that a man should let see his weaknesses, which was the opposite of everything he believed about falling in love.

"Fair enough," she said. "I get scared sometimes, Antonio."

She turned so her back was against the door and she was facing him across the bench seat. She had one leg curled underneath her and her arms crossed under breasts. She hadn't taken the time to change out of her khakis and mission shirt.

He didn't want to talk to her now because he was very much afraid that if he did, he'd make some excuse just to keep her...

"We all do."

"I know that. But the stuff that scares me isn't the stuff that freaks out of most people. I get scared when

I start to care too much about someone. And you know what? I've been really careful about not letting anyone mean that much to me," she admitted.

As always, her honesty cut him to the quick. She might be competitive, but he knew she'd never cheat to win. "I get that."

"I know you do. That's why when I retreat and hurt you… I hate myself for it. Today scared me. I think it scared everyone, but honestly it wasn't the situation— I knew we could handle that. It was afterward when I kept picturing you in Velosi's spot and wondering what I would have done if you had been trapped. Would I have been so calm?"

He suspected she would. Izzy was nothing if not calm in the eye of the storm. She always did what needed to be done. Afterward, she might have shaking hands, but during the event she was cool and calm.

"I felt the same way. But I think we both know that we aren't the type to ever put all that training aside."

"Really?" she asked. "Why are you here, then? What's worrying you?"

"I just wanted to come to the place where you and I were the most honest with each other. I wanted to be in the spot where…where I realized that there was so much more to you than dares and trying to one-up me," he admitted.

Carly had moved back and forth between them, finally settling on Antonio's lap, and he stroked the dog, trying to read Izzy. "Did you think I was here to drink?"

She shrugged, and that tiny gesture hurt more than he had expected it to. She had never seen him in his addiction days so she couldn't know that it wasn't the crutch it once had been. And he also knew that she couldn't be the salvation he'd been thinking she was. Izzy still didn't trust him. Or maybe it was herself she didn't trust, but there was no future where there wasn't trust. Before, he'd been thinking he'd do anything to woo her, but without trust, he was going to have to end this.

He steeled himself to continue. "So… I guess we should probably talk about our relationship and maybe figure out if this is where it ends."

THAT WAS NOT what she'd been expecting to hear. Antonio had always been so solid and, to be honest—fair or not—she'd thought he'd be there as she battled her own fears and tried to figure out how to make this relationship work.

But maybe he was right. Yet, if this was the right choice, then why did her heart hurt at the thought of saying goodbye to him?

"I don't… I mean, if that's what you want," she said. She remembered the few times her mom had tried to keep a relationship going after one of her stepdads had wanted to end it. It never had worked out. Watching it had hurt; she couldn't imagine what living through it had been like for her mom.

Izzy had a moment of clarity about her mother and how hard it must have been to try so many times to find love, only to have it end. Once was hard enough. She couldn't imagine how her mom had done it time and again. And maybe that was exactly why she had decided to spend the rest of her life by herself.

"What do you want?" he asked. "I'm tired of guessing. I tried to be the man you could count on."

"I'm sorry I didn't want to get all cozy and intimate in the locker room," she said, also knowing she wasn't exactly hitting above the belt with that. She'd been the one who had needed to hold him and kiss him. And she realized, as her hands shook a little bit where she had them on her lap, that she was still afraid. Still worried about Antonio. She'd followed him because she loved him and she had no idea what to do about that.

He shook his head. "That isn't what I'm talking about. I know that my kiss…well, our kiss, was too much while we were at work, but afterward just walking away like that. What am I supposed to think?"

"That maybe I'm not you, Antonio. I'm not used to people looking at me and talking about my personal life. You know your call sign is Playboy. I don't want everyone to say that you're the one who thawed the Ice Queen."

Antonio shook his head and looked away from her and out of the truck window. "Is that what this is? You're afraid of gossip. That's not the Bombshell I know. Gossip doesn't affect us if we are sure of our feelings. To be fair I haven't been a playboy for a long time and, Izzy, you aren't the Ice Queen. Not like you were when we were new to the space program. Everyone knows that.

"Are you afraid they might see us falling in love?"

"Love?" she asked.

"Dammit."

Love. Did he love her? What did that mean if he did? Would that change things between them?

"I love you, too," she said. It had slipped out without her meaning to really say it, but there it was. "How's that for truth? I do love you. Today, when I surfaced and saw you I was flooded with that love. I can't deny it anymore."

He turned to her and scooted across the bench seat. Carly scrambled off his lap as he reached toward her. "Do you mean that?"

"I do. But I don't know that it makes any difference in the end," she said. "I'm still going to be me. I'm still not sure how to act around others and I did figure out one thing earlier—I don't want to be the reason you don't go on that first mission."

He dropped his arm and gave her the kind of hard look that would have made a lesser person shiver. "Is that why you followed me here?"

"Yes and no. You confuse me, but I can't just let you go. I don't know if we can really be in a relationship because I'm not good at them and it's only been a short time that we have been together. But walking away from you, watching you not get your dream, that's not something I want to do, either."

She had never been more honest with a man. She had no idea what to expect from Antonio here. But she'd never been the kind of woman to not give something her all, and that had to include love.

If she'd learned anything from being with Antonio, it was that he wasn't going to go back easily into the role of friendly rival. Too much had changed between them and she wasn't going to run from it.

She was afraid that she'd be tempted to give up that first mission for him. Which would probably get her in a lot of trouble. Love had changed her, but she realized that going first wasn't the most important thing. If she could figure out a way to be with Antonio for the rest of her life, then she'd figure out how to make the space program work for them, too. And she knew she didn't have to see marriage and kids in her future, but she did see Antonio and she would continue to for the rest of her life. Neither of them was going to walk away from Cronus. Could they say the same about each other?

"Say something," she said at last.

18

ANTONIO HADN'T BEEN prepared to have this conversation, but then like everything with Izzy it had happened unexpectedly. And maybe that was the problem he'd been having. He'd been trying to make this fit into a mold. The two of them weren't like two average people who were falling for each other.

There was a competitive edge to what they did because of their personalities. And falling for her. "I love you," he said. He hated how raw his voice sounded, but even when he'd been living his life inside of the bottle, he hadn't felt as vulnerable as he did right now. And his hands were shaking.

Dammit.

"I don't know what that means. I don't know if that is what you want to hear or if that's going to drive you away," he said.

"I'm still here," she said. Then she moved, getting up and straddling his lap. She put her arms around his shoulders and he felt her fingers in the hair at the nape of his neck.

She kissed him slowly, with all the passion he remembered from their first kiss in the gym, but this time he felt the love behind it. He knew that she loved him. He wrapped his arms tighter around her, deepening the kiss. They didn't have to figure out the rest of their lives in the front cab of his truck in the parking lot of a roadhouse in Texas.

Her tongue tangled with his and the tightness that had been in his gut finally loosened. He felt he could breathe for the first time since…well, since they'd gone into the simulator this morning.

They had the rest of their lives to figure it out. He just needed to know that she was by his side. He wanted her, needed to make her his and confirm their love with the bonds of the flesh.

He skimmed his hands down her torso, brushing his fingers against the sides of her breasts and holding her close to him before breaking the kiss.

"I thought I lost you twice today," he said, resting his forehead against hers and staring into her eyes.

She blinked and then hugged him tighter again. "Me, too. I didn't know that loving someone could be this hard. You know in movies it always seems like, yay, we're in love, and everything is all rosy and perfect. But this is… Well, it's complicated."

He threw his head back and laughed. "It's damned complicated. My only other experience with love was the destructive side and it led me to a very dark place.

It's so different with you, Izzy. I don't know what I'm doing, either."

"Good. Then we can figure this out together," she said. "We're two of the smartest people I know. We can make this work."

"Yes, we can," he said. "Want to get out of this parking lot and see if they have a room for us at the Grand Hotel?"

"I'd love to," she said.

She scooted off his lap, got out and went to her car. He followed her to the Grand Hotel. She took Carly for a walk in the park while he arranged for a room—the same suite they'd had the last time, with special permission for Carly. It was only as the desk clerk handed him the key that he remembered the present he'd bought for Izzy. He'd left it in his truck.

He went and retrieved it before finding Izzy. She was standing in the town square while Carly sniffed around.

"We got the same suite," he said. "I'll take Carly's leash."

"It's okay, I've got her."

"I know, but I want you to open this," he said, handing her the package.

She took it from him, giving him a quizzical look. "You bought me a present?"

"I've had it for a while. Just was waiting for the right time to give it to you. This seemed like the perfect moment."

She turned the package over in her hands and then opened it. He watched her face as she looked at it. He'd special-ordered the book from a friend of his who did handmade illuminated books. The story was simply hers. It was about a little astronaut girl who had crashed on a ranch in South America and taken a cowboy back into space with her. They explored all of the stars and then, when they were done, returned to Earth. But when she left, she took his heart with her.

"Antonio…this is the sweetest present I've ever received," she said.

"The artist is a friend of mine and I asked her to use *Le Petit Prince* as the story frame," he said. He knew she would like it, but he hadn't realized how much *he* would.

"Thank you."

"You're very welcome," he said.

"Not just for the book but for loving me and making me realize how good life can be when you share it with someone," she said.

Carly bounded back over to them and Izzy took his hand and led him back to the hotel. They went up to their suite and made a bed for Carly in the living room area before Antonio lifted her into his arms and carried her into the bedroom, closing the door behind them.

Izzy's PHONE RANG just as Antonio set her on the bed. She glanced at the caller ID and saw that it was Ace.

"I have to take this," she said.

His phone started ringing a moment later.

She heard him answer his call as she stepped out of the bedroom and into the main living area.

"Hi, Ace."

"Izzy, I'm glad I got in touch with you. We are making a few calls today to give you some news."

Her breath caught in her chest. "Not tomorrow at the meeting?"

"Well, the formal announcement will be then, but Mal and Jose wanted to get the information ready for a press release and I don't like putting names on a list until I've talked to my people."

Everything inside her tensed as she waited. "Okay. So I guess the mission crews have been decided?"

"They have," Ace said. "Mal is going to be the one calling Antonio, since he is part of the Space Now program."

"Fair enough," she said. Honestly, she just needed to know if they had gotten onto the first mission. Both of them. It was taking Ace a long time to make the announcement.

"First of all, let me say that we decided that having couples on the crews wouldn't be a detriment to the mission, and you and Antonio will be deployed together."

"Oh, wow. That's great. Which mission?" she asked.

"The first one. You will be with me, and Hemi is the second-in-command. Bomber and Hennessey are also on your mission, as are Vicki and Dean. Lourdes and Mike are the final two. We increased the crew from five to ten based on what we saw today and yesterday. We will be briefing everyone in the morning. You can talk about this with Antonio and the rest of the candidates if they've spoken to one of us.

"Congratulations, Izzy. I'm really glad to have you and Antonio on my team," he said, before ending the call.

Izzy squealed as she ran to the door and heard Antonio's voice. He was still on the phone.

She stuck her head around the corner of the doorway, glancing in. Antonio had a very serious look on his face as he concentrated on the call.

Then he smiled over at her and beckoned her to come in. She settled onto his lap as he ended his call.

"Did Ace tell you?" he whispered to her.

"Yes! I'm so excited."

"Me, too," he said. "This might be the best day of my life."

She wanted to make it a day he'd never forget, so she pushed him back on the bed and straddled his hips. She reached for the hem of her shirt and ripped it up and over her head. His hands were on her waist, skimming up her back to undo her bra. She shrugged out of it as he undid her pants and shoved them down her legs. She had to roll off him to get them off and took her shoes off, too.

When she turned back to the bed, he'd removed his clothes and had his erection in his hand, stroking it up and down as he watched her. She climbed back onto the bed and straddled him again. His hands cupped her butt as he drew her forward, and the tip of him found her opening easily.

HE STROKED HIS hand from the crown of her head down her back to her waist. His fingers dipped between her legs.

She rubbed her hands over his chest, tracing the line

of hair that tapered slowly down his midriff, and felt the tip of his erection.

There was a tiny bit of moisture there, which she rubbed around the head of his cock. "I want you."

"I want you, too."

He shifted his hips and she wrapped her hand around him, stroking him from the root to the tip. On each stroke she ran her finger over the head and around to the backside of it, where she noted that he shivered each time she touched him.

He cupped both of her breasts this time and she shifted around, keeping her grip on his cock but moving so that he could touch her the way she liked it.

She pushed her shoulders back and watched as he leaned forward. She felt the warmth of his breath against her skin first and then the brush of his tongue. He circled her nipple with it and she tightened her grip on his cock as he closed his mouth over her and suckled her deeply.

She realized what she was doing and loosened her grip a bit, stroking him again until she felt his hips lift toward her, moving in counterpoint to her hand. She reached lower and cupped his balls, rolling them in her fingers before squeezing slightly. He groaned and pulled his mouth from her breast. He gripped the back of her neck and brought her mouth to his.

Then he guided her down against his cock. She didn't move her hand except to enable the tip of his erection to enter her. Just the tip, as she kept that tight grip on his shaft.

She moved her hand down so that he could slide a little more into her. He muttered a Spanish curse under his breath, and she smiled, reveling in both the feel of his thick cock at the entrance of her body and at her power over him. He lifted his head and took her nipple in his mouth again, biting down lightly, and she shuddered.

The time for playing this little game was over as she craved all of him inside of her. Now, she thought.

She moved her hand from his cock and tried to impale herself on his entire length, but he wasn't about to let her have him now. He held her where she'd kept him, with just enough of them connected to drive both of them mad.

She was wet and ready for him and she shifted forward, taking him deep inside. Antonio sat up, making him go even deeper. He wrapped his arms around her, and she had her arms and legs wrapped around him.

He kissed her neck. "You are my everything, Izzy. I never thought I'd find a woman like you."

He rocked his hips and held her completely in his arms.

"You've shown me a side of life I never knew existed," she whispered. "I love you more than I thought I'd ever love anyone. I'm so excited about the thought of spending the rest of our lives together."

"Every night like this," he said.

He whispered in her ear, telling her all the things he was going to do to her as he thrust up into her, filling her completely at last.

She pushed her pelvis forward, trying to take him deeper, but he was already as deep as he could go. His hands found her bare buttocks and he rocked her forward. God, she loved the feel of those big hands against her ass. He parted her cheeks and she felt one finger sliding along her furrow, and she squirmed closer to him.

Every particle in her being craved more of Antonio. She needed him, like the earth needed the sun to help keep it in orbit. His mouth slid from hers, nibbling down her neck and biting her at the base of her neck and shoulder. She shivered and felt everything in her body reaching once again toward climax. But she didn't want to come too soon. She wanted this to last as long as it could.

She dug her fingernails into his shoulders as she rocked her hips harder against him, and when he tightened his hand in her hair and groaned her name, she melted. Her orgasm rushed over her as she kept thrusting forward.

His hips moved faster, and then a moment later she felt a gush of his warmth filling her. She couldn't stop rubbing against him as she coaxed a second orgasm from her body.

His breath sawed in and out, brushing over her sensitized skin as she fell forward. He wrapped one arm around her shoulder and the other around her waist. She shivered and he pulled her closer.

They stayed wrapped in each other's arms for an hour, talking about the mission and the fact that they had worked hard to get where they were and that both had found their dreams in the stars—and in each other.

THE MICK TANNER TRAINING FACILITY was bustling with activity when they arrived the next morning. Antonio took Carly to his room and then joined Izzy in the main briefing room. Everyone seemed more relaxed than they had in a long time.

Velosi had been named the mission commander for the second mission and he was happy to be leading the second phase. The formal announcements were made and everyone was asked to come forward for a group photo. Ace shook his head.

"What is it?" Antonio asked him.

"I was just thinking that this was the one place on earth I couldn't wait to get away from, and it has brought me all of my dreams. Molly and the Cronus missions. How lucky could one man be?"

"Pretty damned lucky," Hemi said, clapping him on the back. "Just like me."

He winked at Jessie, who stood in the corner shaking her head at her fiancé.

Antonio didn't say anything out loud. As he looked over at Izzy, he saw the love in her eyes, and he knew his life was on the path he had always known he would find. He had everything he ever wanted. A life in the stars with Izzy by his side.

* * * * *

Turn the page for a sneak preview of
USA TODAY *bestselling author*
Katherine Garbera's
TYCOON COWBOY'S BABY SURPRISE,
Available May 2017 from
Harlequin® Desire.

A work assignment is about to thrust wedding planner Kinley Quinten back into the orbit of the man who rocked her world...and fathered her secret child.

"**P**ack your bags, kid, we're taking the show on the road," Jacs Veerling said as she swept into Kinley Quinten's office. The term was a stretch for the large workroom she shared with Willa Miller, the other wedding planner who worked for Jacs.

"Who's going on the road? Both of us? All three of us?" Kinley asked.

"Just you, Kin," Jacs said. "I've inked a deal to plan the wedding of reformed NFL bad boy Hunter Caruthers. It's taking place in your home state of Texas and when I mentioned your name, he said he knew you. Slam-dunk for us. I think that might be why he picked our company over one in Beverly Hills."

Caruthers.

At least it was Hunter and not his brother Nate.

"I can't."

Kinley couldn't help the panic rising inside of her. She had no plans to return to Texas.

Ever.

Jacs walked over and propped her hip on the edge of Kinley's desk. "He asked for you. Personally. Will you die if you go to Texas?"

"No. Of course not. But is there anything I can say that will make you change your mind?"

"Not really," Jacs said. "The client wants you and you really have no reason not to go, do you?"

Yes. Nate Caruthers. The man who'd rocked her world for one passion-filled weekend, fathered her child and then interrupted her when she called later with important news, telling her what happened in Vegas needed to stay there. Kinley glanced down at the framed picture of Penny on her desk and felt her stomach tighten. After that disastrous call to Nate, she'd vowed not to allow him to let Penny down the way her own father had let her down.

Nate was her new client's older brother and still lived on the family's ranch outside Cole's Hill.

"No reason. When do I need to start?" Kinley asked.

*What will happen when rich rancher
Nate Caruthers finds out he's a daddy?
Don't miss
TYCOON COWBOY'S BABY SURPRISE
Available May 2017 wherever Harlequin Desire
books are sold.*

Get 2 Free Books,
Plus 2 Free Gifts—
just for trying the Reader Service!

One SEAL can be trouble…but when two sexy SEAL twin brothers return home on leave for a high school reunion, anything can happen!

Read on for a sneak preview of
ONE NIGHT WITH A SEAL.
Enjoy two linked novellas in one book—
"All Out" by New York Times *bestselling author*
Tawny Weber
&
"All In" by RITA® *Award–winning author*
Beth Andrews.

"The Bennett brothers are coming home?"

A thrill of delight shot through Vivian Harris at the news.

"Yep, Xander and Zane should be here—" Mike looked at his watch and grinned "—within the hour."

"Both of them?" At her brother's scowl, Vivian made a show of sweeping her long blond bangs away from her face and giving him a wide-eyed look of concern. "Are you sure Little Creek can handle an invasion by the Bad Boy Bennetts?"

"Probably not," Mike replied with a laugh. "Luckily they're only here for ten days. Other than breaking a few hearts, I don't think they can do much damage with so little time."

"Last time they were only home a week and they got into a huge bar fight after you challenged them to see who could drink the most shots. They broke the table at the diner arm wrestling, and if rumor is correct, they were seen streaking down Main Street at three in the morning as part of some insane decathlon." Oh, how she'd wept over missing that sight.

"Nah, the streaking was just a rumor. But the rest are true." Mike's grin widened. "I'm going to have to do some serious thinking if I'm going to top all of those challenges."

Vivian had a few challenges she wouldn't mind offering Zane. Talk about a dream worth living—if only for ten days.

Her fingers tapping a beat on the scarred surface of the bakery counter, Vivian gave herself a minute to delve into her favorite fantasy. The one that starred her and Zane Bennett covered in nothing but chocolate frosting and a few tempting dollops of whipped cream.

Maybe it was time to try out a few of her dreams on something other than her bakery business. After all, if she could make a glistening penis-shaped cake worthy of oohs and ahhs, how hard could it be to get her hands on Zane Bennett's real one?

Vivian flashed a wicked smile.

Hopefully, once she got her hands on it, it'd be very, very hard.

Don't miss
ONE NIGHT WITH A SEAL
by Tawny Weber and Beth Andrews.

Available June 2017 wherever
Harlequin Blaze books and ebooks are sold.

www.Harlequin.com

HBEXP0517

HARLEQUIN®

A *Romance* FOR EVERY MOOD™

Love the Harlequin book you just read?

Your opinion matters.

Review this book on your favorite book site, review site, blog or your own social media properties and share your opinion with other readers!